S0-CWW-171

"Let's not complicate an already tense situation by playing games," she said.

Grant plucked a flower and, as Nicole went rigid with surprise, threaded it through one of the satin frogs that closed her dress. Her skin, made unnaturally sensitive by his presence, felt the pressure of his fingers as if they were touching her directly.

"Why did you do that?"

"Does there have to be a reason, beyond the beauty of the woman and the beauty of the flower?" Grant's arms tightened around her. "Tell me something. Why are you so afraid of me?"

She could barely see him, but she could feel him all around her, all over her, teasing her senses. Deep down she wanted to play his game. But games had winners and losers. Anybody could tell by looking at Grant Sutton that he had never lost a game in his life. And she had already lost so much...

Dear Reader:

Last month we were delighted to announce the arrival of TO HAVE AND TO HOLD, the thrilling new romance series that takes you into the world of married love. This month we're pleased to report that letters of praise and enthusiasm are pouring in daily. TO HAVE AND TO HOLD is clearly off to a great start!

TO HAVE AND TO HOLD is the first and only series that portrays the joys and heartaches of marriage. Its unique concept makes it significantly different from the other lines now available to you, and it offers stories that meet the high standards set by SECOND CHANCE AT LOVE. TO HAVE AND TO HOLD offers all the compelling romance, exciting sensuality, and heartwarming entertainment you expect.

We think you'll love TO HAVE AND TO HOLD—and that you'll become the kind of loyal reader who is making SECOND CHANCE AT LOVE an ever-increasing success. Read about love affairs that last a lifetime. Look for three TO HAVE AND TO HOLD romances each and every month, as well as six SECOND CHANCE AT LOVE romances each month. We hope you'll read and enjoy them all. And please keep writing! Your thoughts about our books are very important to us.

Warm wishes,

Ellen Edwards

Ellen Edwards
SECOND CHANCE AT LOVE
The Berkley Publishing Group
200 Madison Avenue
New York, N.Y. 10016

Second Chance at Love

STRANGER IN PARADISE
LAUREL BLAKE

**SECOND CHANCE AT LOVE
BOOK**

"What lips my lips have kissed"
by Edna St Vincent Millay
quoted with permission from *Collected Poems*, Harper & Row.
Copyright 1923, 1951 by Edna St Vincent
Millay and Norma Millay Ellis.

STRANGER IN PARADISE

Copyright © 1983 by Laurel Blake

Distributed by The Berkley Publishing Group

All rights reserved. No part of this publication may be reproduced or
transmitted in any form or by any means, electronic or mechanical,
including photocopy, recording, or any information storage and re-
trieval system, without permission in writing from the publisher.

Requests for permission to make copies of any part of the work should
be mailed to: Permissions, Second Chance at Love, The Berkley Publishing Group, 200 Madison Avenue, New York, NY 10016.

First edition published November 1983

First printing

"Second Chance at Love" and the butterfly emblem are trademarks
belonging to Jove Publications, Inc.

Printed in the United States of America

Second Chance at Love books are published by
The Berkley Publishing Group
200 Madison Avenue, New York, NY 10016

For Glenith and Carl Maxwell

STRANGER IN PARADISE

CHAPTER ONE

THE BLUE AND GOLD BAHAMASAIR propjet touched down with a sound like silk tearing. Behind the fence that edged the runway of the Silver Cay, Bahamas Airport, Nicole Starr slowly let go of the railing she had been clutching. Five years. It had been five years since Barry's death, but the sight of an airplane on the wing still tied her in knots. With a cold hand she pushed back her mane of streaky blond hair. *Let it go*, she thought. *Put on a smile. Show Robert what a big girl you are.*

Already the plane had reached the end of the short runway and was turning to taxi back. As she searched its windows for a glimpse of her employer, Nicole wondered again what whim was bringing Robert Gresham to Silver Cay on such short notice. For over four years he had been content to let her run Seawinds, Incorporated, his batik clothing and yard goods firm, with little interference. Seawinds was a sideline, of course, bought to please his first wife. Robert's considerable wealth came

1

from Texas oil and Florida real estate. Two or three times a year, on his way to some sailing event, Nicole could expect him to breeze in for a desultory look at the accounts and maybe to take her fishing, as he had once taken her and Barry. But never before had he come at this time of year, when you could fry your breakfast egg on the hood of the Seawinds station wagon, and when by afternoon the humidity would take the curl out of a pig's tail. Why wasn't he home in Palm Beach, playing golf with famous people?

Steps folded down and the first passengers came blinking into the sunlight. Nicole was nearly knocked off her feet by a mountainous woman in a print turban plowing to the railing.

The crackly phone call from Robert's secretary had been cryptic. "Mr. Gresham wants the workshop and the accounts in strict order. He also said to tell Mrs. Johnson to expect six for dinner on the evening of his arrival. You're to spare no expense on the menu."

"Is he bringing guests?"

"I've booked two seats on Flight 242," the secretary said snippily. "Good-bye, Mrs. Starr."

Nicole stood on tiptoe, craning over a vast calicoed shoulder. Maybe Robert was bringing Cecile, his second wife. That would be a trial. Cecile was a beautiful, restless woman who was always snapping at the employees and telling intricate stories about her wealthy family on the West Coast, where she wished she had stayed. She usually had to be reminded of Nicole's name and then expected Nicole to drop her work and plan excursions for the boatloads of Cecile's friends who would soon follow. Things were much more relaxed when Robert came by himself.

The crowd in front of Nicole shifted and there he was, coming across the tarmac straight toward her, one of a handful of passengers deplaning at Silver Cay. He was apparently alone. Nicole smiled and waved to get his attention, but without success. Robert was like a brother to her. He had been Barry's friend, as well as his employer. Robert was the one person with whom she felt comfortable reminiscing about the old days, when Barry was still alive.

She waved again. Robert was wearing a suit the color of vanilla ice cream and his golden hair shone. His charmingly spoiled features radiated good humor and the attentions of an expensive health club.

Quite suddenly, a taller, darker man with a mustache appeared at his shoulder. Whatever he was saying out of the side of his mouth cast a shadow of worry across Robert's face. What could be wrong? Nicole squinted at them, trying to remember where she had seen the stranger before. In contrast to Robert's dandified executive look, this man wore tight, faded jeans, a white oxford-cloth shirt open at the neck, and old but well-polished brown loafers. He carried a rumpled linen sport jacket slung over one shoulder and, in his left hand, a battered leather attaché case and a rolled-up newspaper. He was deeply tanned and his brown hair had been coarsened by prolonged exposure to sun and salt water. Maybe, Nicole speculated, he was a scuba instructor at the yacht club, the kind that flashes his teeth at sunbathing matrons and makes them want to include him in their wills. Because of the lines in his face she put his age near Robert's, about thirty-five, although his well-muscled body argued for twenty-five. Maybe he was just one of those professional sportsmen her boss was always hiring to take him on to the next expensive thrill: deep-sea fishing, diving, big-game hunting.

As she moved over to the gate they would enter, it amused her to continue comparing the two men. Robert's walk, for instance, was unobtrusively graceful, as if he had been handed walking lessons along with all the other privileges he'd received as a child. Mr. Sports Bum, on the contrary, had a shambling go-to-hell gait that made his broad shoulders swing with lazy arrogance. Oh, yes, she could just see him chatting up the wealthy ladies at the bar of Captain Jack's Yacht Club...

"Nicole!" His face ruddy with surprise and pleasure, Robert sprang ahead of his companion.

"Hi, boss." She held out her hands to him. Robert captured them in one of his and raised them to his lips. But his blue eyes were troubled.

"You didn't have to meet us. I didn't expect you to."

"I wanted to." Nicole smiled up at him, wondering what, if anything, was wrong. She knew him well. His manner toward her was subtly different. But after all it was the first time she had mustered the nerve to come to the airport. That might account for it.

Over Robert's shoulder, shrewd brown eyes watched the exchange. Behind the intelligence in those eyes danced a sparkle of pure devilment.

"Hello. I'm Nicole Starr," she told the man, leaning around Robert to do so.

"Oh, excuse me." Robert turned to the man, slipping an arm around her waist. She didn't exactly mind him doing it, but he had never done it before. "This is Grant Sutton," he said, "a friend and business associate, of whom I'll tell you more later. He'll be joining us for dinner tonight." He nodded to Sutton. "I've told you about Nicole."

"Mrs. Starr." His handshake was firm, his glance raking, the twist of his mouth amused. "I didn't expect the power behind Seawinds to be so lovely. I took you for one of Robert's models."

Nicole pulled back her hand, after he had held it a shade longer than was courteous. "That's all right, Mr. Sutton. I took you for a beach bum." Beach bum, indeed. So this was the formidable Grant Sutton, who had recently been profiled in a leading U.S. business magazine. She hadn't known he was a friend of Robert's.

Sutton chuckled. "It seems that our stereotypes are

showing." The quick eyes went to Robert. "And speaking of stereotypes, I can't say much for your powers of description. From what you said about Mrs. Starr, I expected a little old lady in black, sitting in a rocking chair." He looked from one to the other, as if he was adding one and one and getting three.

"Don't know how you got that idea," Robert said mildly, but his smile was strained. "I'll see about the luggage. Nicole, why don't you take Grant somewhere out of this sun?"

"Wait!" Nicole wanted to suggest that they stick together, but a cart of luggage interposed, and Robert was gone. Reluctantly she turned to face Sutton, all of the questionable things she had read and heard about him crowding to the forefront of her thoughts. Cutthroat business analyst. Champion womanizer. She could think of nothing to say.

His eyes flicked over her, whiplike, returning twice to her loosely cut white slacks of sea-island cotton and the purple and white overblouse batiked with starfishes and sand dollars.

"That's a Seawinds outfit you're wearing?"

"Yes. Do you like it?" She put some challenge in her tone. She didn't like his stare.

Grant Sutton stepped back, folded his arms, and made a more leisurely inspection of her. His gaze bored right through the fine cotton, until she was sure he could see the chicken pox scar on her thigh and the embroidered heart on the hip of her bikini panties.

"Very nice. But too conservative, don't you think?"

"My figure or my clothes?"

His eyebrows shot up. He pulled on an end of his mustache. "The clothes. Believe me, only the clothes."

Nicole flushed. She had walked right into that one. She lifted her chin and tried to look down her nose at him, but he was much too tall.

"Seawinds has built its reputation on simple, classic

resort wear. We don't try to compete with Frederick's of Hollywood."

"Obviously. And you're losing megabucks that way."

"Are you here for business or pleasure, Mr. Sutton?" she asked irritably.

He fanned back a cuff to check his watch. The watch was a Patek Phillipe, the fountain pen peeping from his shirt pocket a Mont Blanc. Apparently the man had taste in some areas, if not in the way he related to women.

"Didn't Gresham tell you?" he asked.

"No."

"I'm here on business. For him. Although"—he favored her with a high-voltage grin—"I wouldn't be opposed to a little pleasure. How about you?"

Well, well. So he was going to be that predictable. "I wish you the best of luck in finding it," she said with lofty calm. "Now if you'll excuse me, I'll see what's keeping Robert." So much for being gracious, she thought flippantly, as she left him standing. But she had met his type before. He was not the first good-looking, footloose male who had approached her, looking for some local action to round out a Caribbean holiday. They wandered through Seawinds by the dozen on guided tours. Besides, if Grant Sutton had come with Robert for the reason she suspected, things were going to get much worse before they got better.

She met Robert returning from the luggage pickup, an overburdened porter struggling in his wake.

Blotting his face with a folded handkerchief, he volunteered, "I invited Sutton to say at the house, but he prefers a hotel. Wants to keep his free time to himself, I guess. I told him we'd give him a lift to the Coral Reef."

"Must we?"

"Why not?"

"I don't like his attitude, Robert. Not at all."

"I wouldn't think of inconveniencing Mrs. Starr," said a sardonic voice.

Nicole whirled guiltily. Sutton, hands in pockets, lounged against a stack of crates not two yards away.

"It's no inconvenience, is it, Nicole?" Robert asked. "It will give us a chance to talk."

But Sutton was already relieving the porter of his suitcases. "We'll talk tonight at dinner," he said reasonably. "I have some paperwork to finish. What time did you say?"

"I'll send a cab around seven," Robert told him.

"I look forward to the evening," Grant replied to him, but his eyes were on Nicole. They were thoughtful as he turned and strode away.

"Independent son of a gun, isn't he?" Robert observed, as they passed straight through the narrow sky-blue building of concrete blocks that served as the Silver Cay air terminal, then out into the waiting babble of competing cab drivers. Sutton sauntered ahead of them, turning his head to take in the women hawking straw goods at the roadside; the posters offering rewards for information concerning pleasure boats missing in Bahamian waters; the long, low horizon frilled with palms and casuarinas. Nicole saw him note in particular the Seawinds station wagon, which she had left directly in front of the terminal steps.

She slid under the wheel, leaving Robert to get the luggage stowed. Tired from sitting up with the accounts the night before, she closed her eyes and let her head fall back against the seat. Through the open window the afternoon sun poured a soothing gold mask over her face and lit an orange glow behind her eyelids. She sighed and sank into the upholstery. The orange glow turned to a cloud of yellow butterflies...

A shadow cut off the sun. Grant Sutton stood at the window.

"Maybe I've led a sheltered life," he said, "but I'm not used to being disliked on sight. I'd like to know why."

Nicole blinked at him. The direct approach, of course. The article in *American Business* magazine had called him tough, savvy, and "aggressive to a fault."

"I've read about you, Mr. Sutton," she said finally, "so I know what you do for a living."

He put an elbow on the window frame and leaned down so that their eyes were on a level. "Tell me."

"I know that you're a self-styled efficiency expert. For an enormous fee you analyze a company, reorganize it, and cut out the fat, so that the company can end up twice as profitable as before."

"Is it the fee that bothers you? That's my price and I'm worth it," he drawled. "What's yours?"

"Well, you know what they say: If you have to ask, then you can't afford it."

His eyes widened with surprise. Then he laughed outright. "You interest me, Mrs. Starr. Maybe I can meet your down payment, anyway."

"To return to your *business* practices," Nicole said severely, "what I don't like is that you ignore the human dimension. You think nothing of sacking twenty-five-year employees if they don't measure up to your standards of efficiency."

"I'm paid to get results. The end justifies the means."

"Not at Seawinds." Looking straight ahead, Nicole gripped the steering wheel with both hands. "You see, Mr. Sutton, if Robert has hired you to take Seawinds apart, then you and I are adversaries. According to my information, you like the adversarial approach. I don't have any apologies to make about the way I've been running things, but your reputation for ruthlessness doesn't exactly make me look forward to working with you."

Out of the corner of her eye she saw him stroke his mustache. "All right, that takes care of the professional side of it. I think you'll find that I'm not at all hard to work with if you have nothing to hide. But what about personally?"

"Personally?" She was perspiring, and not from the sun.

"I offended you."

"Your manner was suggestive." She winced. Spoken like a little old lady in black, sitting in a rocking chair!

"My dear Mrs. Starr, if frank admiration makes you uncomfortable, then it's your problem, not mine. However"—he leaned further in the window—"since I make my living solving problems—"

"Don't give me a line. Being a single woman in a place like Silver Cay, I've heard them all."

"A line, by definition, is a lie. I don't lie. I believe what I say."

"The best anglers always do." Nicole gave him a smile like a thin slice of lemon. "The other Coral Reef guests are getting tired of waiting."

He glanced toward the limousine. "You're right. We'll finish this conversation tonight." Straightening, he added, "As for the article in *American Business,* where you seem to have gotten your opinion of me, it's naive to believe everything you read."

If she only believed half of it, Nicole thought as she watched him walk away, it would be enough to hang him. When the interviewer had asked one of Sutton's girlfriends what sort of recreation Sutton, an amateur sportsman, enjoyed most, the girl had said, "Horizontal."

"Where in the world have you been?" she demanded as Robert slid in beside her and loosened his tie.

"I ran into someone I know. How are you and Sutton getting along?"

Nicole started the engine and threw the car in gear. "How could you bring that barracuda here? How could you hire him without warning me?"

"That bad, is it?" He put a hand flat on the seat to

steady himself as Nicole whipped the wheel left, then right, to free them from the snarl of taxis.

"I just wish I had been consulted."

"Okay, I'm sorry." Robert slapped his pockets for cigarettes. "But there wasn't time. He's in great demand. I had to take him when I could get him."

Immediately in front of them sailed the Coral Reef limousine and, in the center of the back seat, the stiff-necked silhouette of Grant Sutton.

Nicole took a deep breath. "To bring an analyst of his caliber in must mean that you're seriously dissatisfied with my management of Seawinds. Naturally I'm shocked, and—"

"Nicole, Nicole." Robert shook his head. "Don't take it that way. You're the best. The quality of the workmanship has shot up since you took over. Profits are steady. It's just that Sutton has good ideas, and I'd like to see what he can do. You know very well that Bahamian industry tends to be behind the times in technology and marketing. He can give us a fresh perspective. Besides, he's offered to return his fee if profits haven't doubled in a year."

"He's pretty confident of himself."

"Confidence is his middle name, and with good reason. But I'm confident about you, too." He patted her hand. "Cheer up."

"All you have to do is pay him," Nicole pointed out. "I'm the one who'll get the third degree."

Robert gave her his I'm-just-a-bumbling-millionaire smile. "You know I don't have all the details at my fingertips like you do. But it won't be so bad. He's thoroughly professional. Nevertheless, if you don't feel you can handle it..."

"I feel like a broiler hen who's just seen her first barbecue grill. But I'll handle it, Boss. There is nothing in the management of Seawinds that I can't defend." Or was there? She wrinkled her nose in annoyance. People like Robert Gresham and Grant Sutton couldn't understand how threatened she felt because they never had to take any of the heat for their decisions. They were insulated by money and power.

But on the other hand, maybe Amy Pinder, her assistant, was right. "You're only twenty-nine, Nicole," she had said just the day before. "Too much of your emotional energy goes into Seawinds. You ought to have more of a personal life." Maybe Nicole *was* taking this threat to the Seawinds status quo too personally. The man had been hired to do a job, that was all. She began to feel foolish. She should have taken out her irritation on Robert for springing this on her, and not Sutton. She would have to apologize that evening.

The two miles of road between the airport and Crescent Harbour, the only town on Silver Cay, stretched through low, matted forest. Now, as they reached the outskirts of town, traffic grew chancy. Nicole concentrated on maneuvering around bicyclists with crates of chickens teetering on their handlebars, skittery motorbikes, and automobiles nearly as old as she was. But as they turned down Rogers Street, the narrow ribbon that bound the blue boat-flecked harbor, she found time to notice things she had never seen in seven years on Silver Cay. The dockside statue of Woodes Rogers, a figure in early Bahamian history, seemed to be listing to one side. The pastel frame houses lining the shore needed paint. The goats grazing on the grounds of the tiny public library were not quaint at all, but scruffy and ill-kempt. And Rogers Street itself, Nicole fretted: When were they ever going to pave these rutted roller coasters properly? Abruptly, as she went back to watching the limousine ahead, she realized what she was doing. She was judging the place she loved best in all the world through the eyes of a man who made his living by pointing out mistakes.

Irked, Nicole took the turn to Seawinds too quickly. She and Robert bumped shoulders. "Sorry," she mumbled. The limousine bored on toward the high-rent end of the island, its most exasperating passenger deep in conversation with the blonde next to him.

"Are you okay?" asked Robert.

"Why shouldn't I be?"

The fingers of his left hand drummed the seat. "You didn't meet the plane because I was bringing Sutton, did you?"

Nicole stared at him. "Heavens, no. Your secretary didn't say who it was. Anyway, why would I do a thing like that?"

"You might be curious about him. A lot of women are." He chewed his lower lip. "I wouldn't want you to get hurt."

"Gee, I didn't know you cared."

"Of course I care." A flush crept up his incipient double chin. "Just be careful. The only reservation I had about bringing him here concerns you. Frankly, I'm glad you two didn't hit it off."

"Thanks for the warning, but I'm wolf-proof." She was touched by his solicitude. So that was why he had been possessive of her at the airport. It might even be why he hadn't told her Sutton was coming, in a misdirected effort to protect her.

"I guess I shouldn't worry," Robert went on. "You're so sensible and quiet. Not Grant Sutton's type at all. It's just..." he chewed his lip again, "...I was thinking about Barry today."

"So was I," she said quietly.

Satisfied, he veered off into a discussion of his golf game.

Sensible. Quiet. No personal life, Nicole mused. A feeling of great wistfulness stole over her. Not the kind of woman who would appeal to a vital, interesting man. Because Grant Sutton was enormously interesting, perhaps the most interesting man she had ever met. She caught her breath. How could she think such a thing?

How dare she, after what she and Barry had meant to each other? Robert was right. Grant Sutton was nothing but trouble.

They were driving under the arched gateway and down the road she knew best. Across a flat field, the weathered limestone bulk of Seawinds shimmered like a mirage. A former cotton plantation, it had been built by British Loyalists fleeing North America after the Revolutionary War. Nicole loved the spidery, rueful voices of history that still whispered in those corners of the estate that had not been remodeled into workrooms and showrooms for Seawinds, Inc., or living quarters for Robert and herself.

The last tour van of the day passed them as they swung into the circular drive leading to the main wing. Here was the spacious suite that Robert kept for himself, as well as a small apartment Nicole used during the work week, when she didn't have time to go to her beach cottage.

"Good old Mamie," Robert said, waving at the housekeeper, who stood in the doorway. Swinging out of the car, he went ahead to greet Mamie and her husband, Sam, who was coming out for the luggage.

Nicole slowly followed. She could not rid herself of the nagging feeling that Robert was still holding something back from her. His concern about Grant Sutton's impact on her did not quite account for his uneasiness. As she entered the high, cool entrance hall, where the mahogany ceiling fan moved gray light about in somnolent arcs, the grandfather clock was chiming five P.M. Two hours. In only two hours Grant Sutton would walk through that door. From the living room Mamie asked her a question, but she did not answer. Standing in front of the clock, she watched the pendulum swing heavily through her reflection in the glass front. *All right,* she thought to her reflection, *admit it. You've hidden something from Robert, too. Grant Sutton fascinates you. You can't wait to see him again.*

CHAPTER TWO

SEVEN P.M. FOUND Nicole still in her bathrobe, studying the clothes strewn across her bed. *Too conservative, don't you think?* Grant Sutton would smirk at them. She tossed a beige jumpsuit on the heap. Dull, dull, dull. Her batik caftans were colorful, but they swallowed her slender form in their one-size-fits-all folds. She pressed the heels of her hands to her temples. What was happening to her? Male guests had come to Seawinds before. Why did this one affect her like a three-alarm fire?

Tires growled on gravel and she was at the window without realizing she had crossed the room. Two stories below idled the Buick belonging to Claude and Edith Van Zandt, the Seawinds attorneys. Dr. McClain, the sixth guest, was probably with them.

A hundred yards down the drive gleamed a second pair of headlights.

Nicole flew to her closet. From the last coat hanger in the back she snatched the emerald brocade cheongsam.

Barry had bought it in Bangkok when he was in the Air Force, because it matched her eyes. She hadn't worn it in years.

Moments later she was standing in front of her full-length mirror, studying the way her bare, tanned legs showed through the slits at the sides of the straight, street-length skirt. The dress fitted her like a film of crème de menthe. Satisfied, she turned to leave the room; but from the picture frame over the dresser, Barry caught her eye.

He stood beside a Starr Charter Service plane squinting into the sun, his billed cap jaunty on the back of his head. One hand was raised to wave at her, as if he were calling out, *Hey there, honey. Remember me?*

With a twinge, Nicole hesitated, then hurried out the door. All she wanted was a pleasant evening, she argued silently as she descended the stairs. Was there anything wrong with that? No, she answered herself, but was that really all she wanted?

Downstairs, a pleasant blur of conversation, stereophonic strings, and clinking glasses floated out of the living room. Nicole stopped outside the arched doorway and peered in.

They sat in a semicircle around the beaten-brass coffee table where Mamie had laid out the hors d'oeuvres. As always, Claude and Edith sat side by side. With his gray cowlick flaring and his tie askew, Claude gave his usual impression of having just stepped from a train wreck. Edith, in a straightforward manner that was unfailingly endearing, looked like a happy potato draped in voile. They were the most compatible couple Nicole had ever known. Robert, looking more relaxed than when he arrived, was keeping them in stitches with some tale of executive high jinks. That left the other two guests to themselves; from the look of things, they liked it that way.

Grant Sutton sat sprawled in one of the barrel-shaped

wicker chairs, cradling a tumbler of rum punch on his belt buckle. The hair of his chest curled into the open neck of his pale blue shirt, and the way he sat, left ankle balanced on right knee, pulled the tan slacks of his casual suit across the muscles of his thighs. But to Nicole's surprise, his partner in conversation was not the good Dr. McClain. It was Amy Pinder, Nicole's assistant, her best friend, and the most incorrigible flirt in the islands.

With a little sigh Nicole thought of all the time she had spent deciding what to wear. With Amy there, she could have worn a refrigerator and nobody would have noticed. Amy, dark and petite, was shaped like a champagne glass. Or, as one of her boyfriends, a French oceanographer, put it, *Elle à le monde sur le balcon,* she has the world on her balcony. Tonight Amy's balcony was barely supported by her low-cut, spaghetti-strapped dress; and the way she leaned toward Sutton reminded one and all that every balcony needs its Romeo.

"Hello, everybody. Sorry I'm late."

As Nicole entered the room she had the eerie sensation that everything was slowing down. The Van Zandts turned, spoke, smiled. Amy waved. Robert came toward her with the heavy movements of a man swimming in quicksand. He had a frozen look of—was it alarm?—on his face. It was taking her forever to cross the room. Or did it just seem like forever because of the way Sutton, who had risen slowly to his feet, was devouring her, inch by inch, with his eyes? When she smiled uncertainly at him, he winked.

Almost at the same time, Robert reached her with a peck on the cheek, and everything sped up to normal again.

"Dr. McClain had an emergency," Robert told her. "Fortunately, Amy found time for us in her busy schedule."

"Now, Mr. Gresham, you know I always have time

for a good time," Amy teased. "And I've already promised to see that Grant doesn't run out of things to do
outside working hours."

"Oho!" cried Edith. "You won't have a minute's rest,
Mr. Sutton. Amy is a girl who keeps her promises."

"When it comes to fun, anyway," Amy said with a
twinkle before someone else brought up the two en-
gagements she had broken off.

"I have no doubt of it," Sutton said with a gracious
nod, but the look he shot at Robert was cold and cal-
culating.

Curiosity and apprehension swirled inside Nicole.
Something was going on beneath the surface of the evening.

A seat had been left for her on the sofa next to Robert.
She sat down and accepted a glass of punch.

"You were the one who uncovered the embezzlements
at the Scott Distillery in San Juan, weren't you?" Claude
was asking Grant. "That was a shrewd piece of work on
your part."

"The scheme got too complicated for anyone to keep
track of." Sutton shrugged. "They started making mistakes, and I caught them."

"Well, you needn't expect to uncover a scandal here,"
Edith declared heartily. "Nicole will defend the honor of
Seawinds!"

Grant Sutton raised his glass to Nicole. "To honor,"
he said and drank, watching her over the rim.

"Hear, hear," Claude intoned, and glasses went up
all around.

The nape of Nicole's neck prickled. She could not
tear her eyes away from Grant's. He almost seemed to
be sending her some private message. She didn't want
to know what it was, then she did, then she didn't again . . .

Abruptly she turned to Robert. "I hope we're not going
to start talking shop. How is Cecile these days?"

Robert told her, but she didn't hear a word. All her

senses were tuned to Grant, who was again bantering with Amy. Even though Nicole was not looking in his direction, the restless source of energy across the coffee table kept pulling at her, until she felt like a helpless asteroid captured into orbit around a massive, unknown planet. When Mamie announced dinner, she started out of her chair with relief.

Amy joined her in the drift toward the dining room. Nicole made her voice light. "Hi, kid. Having fun?"

"What do you think?" Amy whispered. "Robert didn't call me until five thirty and I had to break another date, but boy, am I glad I did!" She glanced over her shoulder and lowered her voice further. "We're going to take a picnic to Shell Cay next weekend. Nothing this exciting has happened here since somebody put the shark in the Palm Courts swimming pool! What do you know about him?"

In the face of such confidence, Nicole's timid hopes collapsed. When Amy went after a man, she always got him. There certainly was no use in competing with her. Besides, Amy had a very uncomplicated view of romance: easy come, easy go. She was just what Sutton was looking for.

"I know he's looking for action," Nicole finally replied.

"How do you know that?" Amy clapped a hand to her mouth. "Oh, Nicole. I wasn't thinking. If you're already interested—"

"Not at all. He isn't my type." How could she ever have thought he was? He had not been sending signals to her. She had only wished he was. And the slinky dress she was wearing was out of character for her. She had never felt comfortable in it. Now she felt stupid. No wonder Robert had looked so surprised when she came in.

The dining table was as big as an ice rink, and six people did not begin to fill it up. The name cards for

Amy and Grant were at the opposite end of the table from Nicole's.

"How nice that they've put us together." Amy glowed at him as he pushed in her chair.

Grant leaned down until his cheek nearly touched hers. "Very fortunate," he murmured.

Nicole busied herself with straightening her silverware. At least she wouldn't have to worry about Grant handing her any more lines. He and Amy were too busy baiting hooks for each other.

"Mamie and I decided on a typical Bahamian menu," she explained when they all had plates of peppery conch chowder in front of them.

No one appeared to notice that those were the last words she said. Robert and the Van Zandts had never been so full of funny stories. Grant Sutton revealed a talent for the sly comment that, once delivered, hung in the air like a ticking time bomb until someone got the point and the room exploded in laughter. And Amy was positively geishalike in her devotion to her dinner companion. Nicole had never seen her work so hard at pleasing a man. Gradually, as the evening wore on, she felt her pre-Sutton calm return. As the passage of a great fish will roil the ocean floor, so had his arrival on Silver Cay disturbed her, she reflected. But now she was sinking back into the dim clarity of her little corner of the ocean, where great fish never came twice. It was quiet there. Peaceful.

Over the last crumbs of the fresh lemon tart, Sutton's voice shattered her serenity. "Tell me," he said to the table at large, "what are the usual after-dinner activities on Silver Cay?" He looked hopefully from one to the other. "Bridge, by any chance?"

"Grant Sutton, you are my friend for life!" Edith exclaimed. "Robert, how clever of you to bring us a new player." She turned back to Sutton. "You see, Claude, Robert, and I are compulsive players, but Nicole doesn't play at all. Usually Dr. McClain is our fourth, but of course he isn't here tonight. And you don't play, do you, Amy?"

"I played in boarding school, but I don't mind sitting out with Nicole."

"Fine," Edith said quickly, the glitter of the addict in her small eyes. "Here or in the sun room?"

"The sun room it is," Robert replied. As people started for the door, he said to Grant, "We play short club. Do you?"

"I don't play at all."

Everyone halted.

"What?" barked Claude.

"I merely asked if you good people played, and I seem to have started a stampede."

"Oh no!" Edith's face looked like a fallen cake.

"But since Amy plays," Grant resumed, "please enjoy your game. I haven't seen the rest of Seawinds, and I'm sure Nicole can show me around."

The skin over Robert's cheekbones tightened. He raked a hand back from his forehead, ruffling his hair up in little spikes. With his head thrust forward, he looked like an irate chicken. "Absolutely not. We can't exclude the guest of honor from—" But the rest of his words were drowned out by the wails of the other three.

"Come on, Mr. Gresham," Amy begged, taking his arm. "I simply adore bridge. But what is a short club?"

In seconds, Nicole and Grant were alone.

"Amy happened to mention who played and who didn't." He grinned. "Clever?"

"It was." Nicole laughed. "But are you that anxious to see your office?"

He held open one of the double doors leading outside. "Of course not. I'm that anxious to get you alone. We have a conversation to finish, remember?"

Seawinds was built in a quadrangle, around a court-yard filled with citrus trees and flowering shrubs. The cicadas fell silent as Nicole started across the shadowed square, her head down. Sutton was a deeper patch of shadow beside her.

"Let's not complicate an already tense situation by playing games," she said at last. "You and I are going to see enough of each other in the office for the next few days. If you want a good time, Amy has volunteered. Or"—her voice cooled several degrees—"you might even try doing without a good time."

"That's what you do, isn't it?"

"I can't see that it's any concern of yours." She stopped and pointed ahead. "The offices are there, at the end of the north wing. The entire east wing is taken up by the workshop, and —"

He stepped in front of her, blocking her view. "Do you really think I came out here to look at this place in the dark, when I can see it much better tomorrow morning?"

She swallowed. The man was a genius at making her feel idiotic. "No, I guess not."

"Good." They were standing beside a bank of hibiscus, where yellow blossoms glowed like votive lights. Grant plucked a flower and, as Nicole went rigid with surprise, threaded it through one of the satin frogs that closed her dress, just below her collarbone. "I came out here to be alone with you, as I said." He adjusted the flower. Her skin, made unnaturally sensitive by his presence, felt the pressure of his fingers as if they were touching her directly. "There." He stepped back.

She touched a petal with one finger. The velvet nap felt alive. "Why . . . did you do that?"

"Does there have to be a reason, beyond the beauty of the woman and the beauty of the flower?"

"There's a bench over there. We can sit down," she said hurriedly, and turned away. The next thing she knew she was pitching forward, as her toe caught on a flagstone. With a gasp she flung her arms wide. At the same instant Grant leaped to catch her. There was a shock of collision and Nicole found herself awkwardly wrapped around him, leaning into him so hard that his belt buckle cut into her midriff. The pit of her stomach swirled.

"Sorry," she stammered, struggling to straighten up. "You'd think I'd know every stone in the place by now." She let go of him. But he did not let go of her. His palms moved over her back. "I'm all right," she said sternly and tried to back away.

His arms tightened around her. "Tell me something. Why are you so afraid of me?"

"I'm not."

"You're trembling."

"It was the fall."

"You were trembling before that, when I gave you the flower."

"Let me go."

"Let you go? After you threw yourself at me?"

"Let me go or—or . . ." It would sound too Victorian to say "I'll scream."

He gathered her closer. "Do you know what I think of every time I see you? A butterfly. A beautiful butterfly, poised to fly away at the slightest word or movement from me. Don't fly away, Nicole. There's nothing to be afraid of."

His mouth and eyes were pools of shadow, but the planes of his face were silvered with moonlight. The silver light broke into sparks in his chest hair and highlighted, against his shirt, the swells of her breasts under the shiny brocade. His body was as hard as hickory wood, but much warmer. A pleasurable ache began to radiate through her. But it was absurd to feel anything! If she had been able to play bridge instead of Amy, he would be saying these things to Amy now.

"I won't fly away," she promised, "if you'll just let me go."

"Hmmm. All right. For now."

The best thing to do, she thought as she collapsed in a huddle on the bench, was to be honest with him. Then he would see that he was wasting his time.

"I'm not afraid of you," she repeated, "I'm just not what you're looking for. Seawinds takes all of my time. I even take work home at night. I like it that way. I have no interest in brief affairs. Or long ones."

He laced his fingers around a knee and leaned back against the palm tree behind them. "You've gotten these turnoffs down to a fine art, haven't you?"

"I'm just being frank."

"You talk turnoff, but the rest of you is a total turn on: your face, that mane of hair, your figure, your walk, not to mention that sensational dress."

"The dress was a mistake."

"I doubt if anyone held a gun to your head and made you wear it. You know what I think? I think that inside the prim little suit of armor that you've constructed out of words there's a very sexy lady struggling to get out."

"It hardly matters what you think." She pressed her knees together, hard. Why couldn't she stop trembling? "If you don't believe I'm telling you the truth about myself, ask Robert."

"I don't have to ask Robert. I already know that you two have your stories matched up."

"What do you mean by that?"

"When we were negotiating the terms of my job here, he fed me the same tale about this dull, widowed manager of Seawinds, who was a workaholic and who had about as much sparkle a brick. When I stepped off the plane and saw you this afternoon, my God, saw and talked to an intense, beautiful, intelligent woman, I asked myself one question: Why did Robert lie to me, and at such length? The man isn't stupid and he isn't blind."

Nicole frowned. Did Robert really think she was dull? "Just what are you getting at?"

"A theory I have. It answers the question of why

Robert described you as he did. How long have you known him?"

"Seven years. And may I point out, before you theorize too much, that I've known you less than seven hours? My husband used to work for Robert before we started Starr Charter Service. In fact it was Robert who suggested that this part of the islands needed more air service. We moved out here just after we were married. Robert was at Seawinds more often in those days. Whenever he was here, we got together with him and his first wife. After he divorced her and married Cecile, it was usually just Robert who came." She balled her hands into tight fists in her lap. "I don't know why I should tell you any of this."

"I understand that your husband's plane crashed off Andros in a tropical storm, about five years ago."

"Yes."

"I'm sorry." He shifted his shoulders against the tree. "And then?"

"And then I didn't know where to turn. I don't know how I could have put my life back together if it hadn't been for Robert. He gave me a job. He has always been very supportive."

"Has he been in love with you from the beginning, or did that come later?"

She stopped breathing. "What?"

"It's obvious, from the way he looks at you, from how possessive he is, from—"

"Robert is a married man!"

"And not the first with a wandering eye."

The cicadas were roaring like lions.

"That's . . . crazy." She faltered. "Robert is my friend. He was Barry's friend. And he has never approached me except in friendship. He's had plenty of opportunities over the years, if he'd wanted to. How do you explain that?"

"He's probably been in love with you for so long that

concealing it has become second nature. I know him better than you think. We've met several times over the years. Just because he has money it doesn't follow that he has courage. Some men aren't capable of reaching out and taking what they want."

"But you are, I suppose."

"I am."

"Oh, I believe it. I had you pegged for a 'taker' the minute I saw you," Nicole snapped. "Tell me, is this the way you repay all of your employers? By stabbing them in the back?"

He sat up and turned toward her, his thigh brushing hers. A wave of dizziness broke over her like music. "Tomorrow at nine I start working for Gresham. Tonight, I'm working for me."

"And working fast, too." She stood up. "I've heard quite enough. Robert was right to warn me about you."

"So he *is* playing dog in the manger." He caught her hand with a soft laugh. "Stay, butterfly."

She tried to wriggle her hand free. "We've been gone a long time. Amy will be wondering what happened to you."

His fingers moved up to her wrist. "So you want to throw Amy at me too."

"Throw Amy at you?"

"Sit down."

Something in his voice made her obey.

As he spoke, his thumb and forefinger took hold of her wedding band and began to rotate it around and around her finger, as if it were a combination lock he wanted to open.

"When Robert sent the cab for me tonight, he sent Amy in it."

"What's wrong with that? He was just providing her with transportation."

His fingers were long and strong. The wedding band kept turning, turning. "I'm not so sure that was his only intention. She arrived with instructions that we get acquainted over drinks in the hotel bar, at Robert's expense. Now, don't misunderstand me. Amy is a lovely woman. I enjoyed it. And I don't think she had any idea that she might be being used. But when we arrived here tonight, I think your boss was half surprised to see us."

It took a moment for his insinuation to sink in. Then Nicole gasped.

"You are a rude and vulgar man! Amy is my best friend. And Robert is not a procurer!" She wrenched her hand away. As she did so, her ring slid off. It rang on the stone walkway once, twice, and was still.

"Oh no!" She dropped to her knees, sweeping her palms frantically over the stones.

Without a word he knelt beside her in the deep shadows, searching too. Twice their shoulders collided, setting her nerves a-jangle. The scent of his aftershave wrapped her in musk and cedar. She could barely see him, but she could feel him all around her, all over her, teasing her senses. This was like a child's silly game, she thought distractedly, a mad combination of blindman's buff and button, button, who's got the button. Hysteria tickled at her. Games. She had told him she didn't want to play games. But hadn't the whole conversation been a game, played by his rules? And deep down, she wanted to play. It was just that she was so afraid. Yes, he had been right about that. Games had winners and losers. Anybody could tell by looking at this man that he had never lost a game in his life. And she had already lost so much. Damn it, where was the ring?

His hand, reaching blindly, caught her by the waist. "There you are. I've found it."

"Thank goodness!"

"Come here."

They were kneeling. Grant pulled her around in front of him. All at once the night air was heavy with cere-

mony. He took up her left hand. She wore her wedding
ring on her right hand, as was the custom for widows in
her family. He must have noticed this when he had held
her hand before. But he spread out the fingers of her left
hand, very deliberately, and slipped the golden circle on
the fourth one. His head dipped, the moonlight flowing
now over his hair, and his lips brushed hers.

"There," he said huskily. "No harm done." He raised
her to her feet.

Nicole stood in a daze. This man was a stranger. It
was impossible to feel anything for him. Yet somehow,
for a moment, when he had placed the ring on her finger,
she had felt a joining, a sharing. Had he felt it, too?

Change rattled as he thrust his hands in his pockets.
He cleared his throat as if embarrassed. The spell was
broken. She remembered what they had been talking
about.

Unsteadily she said, "I don't suppose it ever occurred
to you that it's your reputation with women that might—
I say *might*—have made Robert want to protect me, and
not his own romantic interest in me."

"I told you before, you've got the wrong idea about
my reputation. No, that's not what it was. It's the attraction between you and me. He senses it. So did I, the
instant we met. So did you. And it scared you silly." He
stepped through a bar of moonlight. He was much closer
than she had thought. "It could be a good two weeks for
both of us. Let me help you get out of that armor, Iron
Butterfly."

He was as smooth as glass. The incident with the ring,
as much as it had moved her, had surely been calculated.
"Don't you think I can see what you're up to?" she asked
sadly. "You pretend to be interested in me as a person,
when all you really want is to find out who you can
depend on for amusement while you're here."

When he didn't answer at once, she found herself

silently imploring him to deny it.

But he said, "I admit it, up to a point. And you ought to admit that you could do with a little amusement."

Nicole stood taller. "I'm only going to say this once, *Mr. Sutton*. When I see you in these offices tomorrow, I expect you to stick to the task for which you were hired. Good night." With as much dignity as she could command, she left him.

How glad she was that she had not apologized for her behavior at the airport! Grant Sutton was a vicious, self-centered liar. He had to be. What could Robert possibly have told the man that had allowed him to come to such a monstrous conclusion? Robert, in love with her even when Barry was alive? It was preposterous! And yet, and yet... She recalled a day, over a year before, when a young attorney friend of Cecile's had wanted to take Nicole for a picnic on a neighboring cay, alone. Robert had protested so vigorously, for some reason Nicole could not recall, that the man had backed off in alarm. And then there was Robert's uneasiness at the airport and in the car, and again when he'd found himself trapped into playing bridge. She shook her head. No. If Robert was so worried, why hire Grant at all? The company was doing fine. She glanced back but could not see her tormentor. Furthermore, she went on arguing, the idea of sending Amy to sidetrack Grant was appallingly cynical. Except, of course, that Amy's propensity for forming quick attachments was well-known. And except for the fact that Amy had never been invited to one of Robert's dinners before. Nicole had assumed it was because she didn't pull enough rank in the company...

The lights lining the courtyard flooded on. Robert hurried toward her.

"What are you doing out here in the dark?"

"I...was just coming inside."

"It's about time. Mamie's serving coffee." He stopped

in front of her, searching her face. "Is anything wrong?"

Was she flushed? Was her lipstick smudged? She ducked her head.

"Why no. A cup of coffee sounds wonderful."

Robert fell in step beside her. "Where's our friend?"

"Oh, I don't know. Enjoying the night air."

He put a hand on her shoulder. "Do you know what I just found? I was looking through the record cabinet and I ran across an old Mel Tormé album. Do you remember the one? It was Barry's favorite. I'll play it for you."

Nicole's steps slowed. "That's the fourth time today you've mentioned Barry. Once in the car, twice at dinner, and now. Why is that?"

His eyes widened. "Don't we always talk about him? I hope the day never comes when you forget him. He was the finest man who ever lived."

"No, no, of course I won't. I don't know what I was thinking of."

A footstep made them turn.

"How goes the bridge game?" Grant asked his host. His eyes were as cold and hard as marbles.

CHAPTER THREE

NICOLE SHOVED THE stack of papers away and leaned back in her desk chair. It had been the longest week of her life. Her head ached with fatigue and her eyes burned. Grant Sutton had pried into every facet of Seawinds, from the cost of paper clips to the chemical composition of the fabric dyes. He had grilled her about every decision she had ever made. She had to admit the man was very good at his job. If she hadn't been on the receiving end of his skilled criticism, she cheerfully would have admired him. As it was, she could only look forward to the day when he handed in his report and left.

She sat up, propping her elbows on her desk and letting her head hang forward, so that she could massage the back of her neck with both hands. At any rate, he had not made any more personal remarks. Their exchanges had been coolly civil and restricted to business, although sometimes he had been so exceedingly formal that Nicole had suspected he was making fun of her.

Amy, true to her word, had kept him entertained. Each noon the two of them headed to the beach for a swim, while Nicole ate a sandwich at her desk and kept working to stay ahead of Grant's demands for information. Amy said he was fun. Hah. A circus was fun. Grant Sutton was a royal pain. And here she was, still at her desk at six-thirty on a Friday evening, with no end in sight. Everyone had gone home but Grant and herself. Robert had left the island two days before, bound for a business meeting in Miami. Ordinarily Nicole would be starting a relaxing weekend at her beach cottage, but the previous day Grant had mentioned the possibility of working straight through Sunday.

She allowed herself the luxury of a small groan.

"Tired?"

Grant stood in the doorway between their offices, rolling down his shirtsleeves.

"I'm exhausted." She sat back, massaging a shoulder. "Do you always drive yourself like this? Seven days a week?"

"Sometimes eight." His brow furrowed. "You *are* tired, aren't you? Delia says I don't realize how hard I push people." He came into the room buttoning his cuffs.

"Delia?"

"My sister."

"It's nice to know you have a sister. It makes you seem more—"

"Human?" He came around her desk. Leaning his hips against the edge, he folded his arms and waited.

"Well, I usually think of ogres as being only children, don't you?"

Grant studied her pleasantly. The spark of mischief that had danced in his eyes at their first meeting was there again. What was he up to? He looked comfortable enough to stay there all night, making her uncomfortable.

"Did you have a question?" She gestured toward the stack of papers.

"Yes. Will you have dinner with me?"

Her eyes fluttered to his and away.

"It's reggae night at the Coral Reef. Look at me, Nicole."

She looked.

"I have reservations. For two."

To gain time for thought, she had a coughing spell. Now she could admit to herself that this was what she had been waiting for—for him to call her hand in the game of impersonality she had forced them to play. How many times that week had she swallowed the bitter taste of regret without naming it! Maybe for him this was only a casual dinner invitation. But for her it opened new possibilities.

Stilling her cough, she pushed back her chair and stood up. "I can't remember the last time I went dancing. I'd love to go."

"Fine." He took a step toward her and made a sweeping motion toward the door. "Shall we?"

Neither of them moved. They were standing very close together.

"We're going now?"

"Now."

"You're a very sudden man."

His eyes swept her from head to foot and returned to her lips. "It's the ogre in me."

She looked down at their toes, inches apart. "I suppose Amy was busy."

"Amy?"

"I just assumed . . ."

He cupped her chin in one hand and tilted her face up. "You assumed wrong. I made the reservations for you and me." His thumb stroked her jaw.

The room sang with stillness. There were threads of gold in his mustache. His lips were full yet finely sculpted, with a dimple at one corner, put there by a faint smile. Her own lips softened and parted slightly.

Heart pounding, she turned back to her desk. "I'll just get the keys and lock up. You can get the lights in your office. Are you as hungry as I am?"

"Yes," he said with strange emphasis. "Starved."

They took the rental car Grant was using. Nicole directed him to the ocean road on the eastern side of the island, avoiding town. For the five-minute drive, they traded pleasantries about island life. But with every second that passed, Nicole became more sure that during the week of carefully maintained distance, something, though she wasn't sure what, had been developing between them, like a Christmas cactus blooming in darkness.

Then they were rounding the mass of sea grape trees on Spanish Point. Straight ahead lay the Coral Reef Hotel, blazing like a hundred-candle birthday cake. Five minutes more and they were crossing its glass-and-brass lobby, through the usual mixture of guests dressed for dinner; sunburned latecomers from the beach, still in bathing suits; and yacht people who had come ashore for drinks in the famous Junkanoo Bar.

Nicole waved at Big Red, the bartender and a local character.

"Evenin', Mrs. Starr." he called. "Nice to see you out on the town! You two stop by later for a drink on Big Red, you hear?"

"If the bartender buys you drinks, you must come here often," Grant joked.

"No, I don't. That's why he's making such a big deal of it. He's always teasing me about being a hard-working executive."

At the entrance to the dining room, the hostess glided forward. "Good evening, Mr. Sutton. Your table is ready, if you'll follow me." Her smile broadened. "Why, Mrs. Starr. It's so nice to see you."

"Are you famous?" he asked, as they followed the woman.

"In a place this size, everybody's famous for something." She felt a giddy rush of elation at being seen with him. The pressure of his hand at the small of her back was unmistakably possessive. She liked it, liked the reckless feeling that his touch ignited in her.

"And what are you famous for?" he whispered in her ear.

A thrill shot down her spine. "For being accompanied by such an attractive man," she replied, giving him a sidelong glance through her lashes.

His arm slid around her. "If anybody's looking at me, it's only out of jealousy," he said, his breath stirring a curl at her cheek.

She smiled up at him, hoping she looked carelessly pleased. But inside she was singing with a sudden joy. The image of a butterfly bursting from a cocoon flashed through her mind.

In the intimately dark dining room, the tables and potted greenery were spaced for privacy. Grant had reserved a window table facing the ocean. When they were seated beside each other in high-backed rattan chairs, Nicole could imagine them alone in a candlelit grotto. Before them, as far as the eye could see, black sky and black water mated with ferocious abandon. As she sat quietly, letting him study the menu and choose the dinner, the sound of the waves had never seemed so simultaneously ancient and fresh. For an instant, without knowing why, she was poised on a knife edge between melancholy and jubilation. Then he said her name. She turned toward him, stirred by a grateful gladness that he was there. Something almost sad moved in the depths of his eyes and his fingers interlocked with hers. An emotion she could not name passed between them.

Awed by her own honesty, she said slowly, "Things are washing over me—feelings, odd thoughts—like those waves out there. I don't know what's happening tonight."

"Don't you?" He squeezed her hand, not like the man

she feared he was, but like the man she wished him to be: a man to lean on, to trust. "It's all right. You'll sort it out in time."

Time? What did this transient stranger mean by offering her time?

Just then a waiter appeared with glasses and a bottle in a bucket of ice.

"Champagne!" she exclaimed, shattering the bittersweet moment.

"I'm celebrating a special occasion," he said with the old, suspect smoothness. "I hope you'll join me."

"Of course."

The waiter popped the cork. There was a rustling from nearby tables as people took notice.

When they had been handed frothing glasses, he continued, "I've just assumed the presidency of a new organization. It's a position that carries with it enormous influence, which I intend to use—but not abuse—to the fullest. I'm fortunate to be given the opportunity."

Bewildered but game, Nicole lifted her glass. "A toast to President Sutton. Congratulations." She knew just enough about champagne to appreciate the elegant, tickling dryness of his choice. "What's the name of this organization?"

He smoothed his mustache with a thumbnail. "The Save-Nicole-From-Herself Foundation."

"What?"

"Its sole function is to prevent you from working too hard. I'm holding several meetings over the next few days."

"You rascal, that's very patronizing!" But she had to laugh.

"I meant it to be. I intend to patronize you every chance I get from now on. You know, you're beautiful when you're not angry."

She watched bubbles rising in her glass. "I guess I haven't been very friendly."

"Maybe I was too friendly in the beginning. How about starting over?"

"All right. Why don't you tell me everything about you that the magazine article left out."

"You remember that damned story remarkably well, considering that it came out six months ago, and considering that it was unlikely we would ever meet."

"Oh, you know how some reading will stick in the mind and some won't. There doesn't seem to be any rhyme or reason to it."

For a time they drank and watched the ocean in companionable silence. The first course of the dinner he had ordered, a delicate crab soup, arrived. It *was* strange how much she remembered, Nicole confessed to herself as they began to eat. The magazine ran a profile of a different business figure each month. Grant's was the only one that had ever captured her fancy. Of course, she had heard of him before that. His business reputation had been forged in the Caribbean basin.

"To begin with," he resumed, "my family is in textiles in North Carolina. It's a moderately successful operation. After my father retired, my sister and her husband took it over."

"Why not you?"

"At the time I was too much of a maverick. I wanted to build or buy something for myself, not take over what the family had made. And I was too restless to settle down. Still am."

"Home is where you hang your hat?"

"I don't even own a hat."

Nicole lifted her spoon, then lowered it again. "You certainly have made a glamorous life for yourself. One month you're in Jamaica, the next in Venezuela. You know all sorts of people and you're always in demand. You have money, companionship, new experiences." She shook her head in admiration. "I sometimes feel that life has passed me by." She stopped, realizing what she had said. "Now say, 'I told you so.'"

He gave her a straight look, but said nothing.

"I didn't mean to let it pass me by," she finished. "It just sort of happened while I was at work."

"There's more than one way of missing out on life. You can be moving too slowly, or too fast. The latter cost me a marriage."

She nodded, recalling mention of a divorce.

"It was my post-divorce activities that the magazine concentrated on, to make a good story. A cheap piece of work."

"Did you consider asking for a retraction? Or suing?"

He swallowed champagne and looked out to sea with fleeting merriment. "Unfortunately they slanted the truth, but they didn't lie. 'Live it up and then live it down.' I was an angry man then. I'm not like that now."

She became interested in her soup again. "If you don't mind my asking, was it this anger that broke up your marriage?"

"What you mean is, did I run around on Risa?" He stared at the hand around his champagne glass. "No. The anger came later. Ours was the opposite problem: lack of emotion. Both of us were more committed to our careers than to each other. We traveled so much and saw each other so infrequently that staying married finally became pointless."

"What about love?"

He was silent awhile. "What we thought was love, wasn't. I haven't seen Risa in years. She's remarried and lives in Hawaii." His face closed up and he concentrated on his plate.

Grant was easier to talk to than she had expected, and much more open about himself. But was this really just a supersmooth line? The man shows himself to be mildly vulnerable so that the woman, feeling less threatened, lets down her defenses? But even as she silently accused him, Nicole knew that only her own fear of his tremen-

dous charm had built this labyrinth of suspicion, and not
Grant himself. Besides, his new, somber mood was obviously sincere.

The soup went away, the cracked-conch dinner arrived, and still he stayed with his thoughts. Why had she
questioned him about his marriage? Nicole fretted. Amy
would have kept the mood light and flirty.

When she couldn't stand another second of silence
she said, "I know that Robert should be the first to receive
your recommendations for Seawinds, but what do you
think of us, in general?"

He blinked like a man dragged from a dream. "It's a
fine little company. I looked at the figures from before
your time and it's obvious what a difference your management has made." He cocked an eyebrow at her. "Too
bad you don't own the place. I'll bet you could do even
more."

"It's something I've thought about. More than you
know."

"Have you talked to Robert?"

"No. Even though he doesn't take much interest in
the company, he wouldn't give it away. Your analysis
has probably given you an idea of a fair asking price."

He nodded.

"I don't have that kind of money. When I sold off the
assets of Starr Charter, I bought a beach cottage on the
other end of the island. What was left over doesn't begin
to be enough."

"I wonder why he hasn't given or sold you shares,
considering what you've done for him." He pushed away
his plate like a man making an aggressive chess move.

"If this is going to be another critique of Robert, I
don't want to get into it. You'll have to admit you were
wrong about him. Otherwise, he wouldn't have left."

"He'll be back."

She stared out the window, feeling the intimacy of
the evening slip away. On the long slope to the beach,

torches flickered in the trees.

"There are only two areas of Seawinds that need substantial improvement," Grant said, returning to the original subject, "but those are crucial: design and marketing. More advertising, more exporting, and some younger styles. Those are all the things we're not going to talk about tonight." He pushed back his chair. "The Save-Nicole-From-Herself bylaws forbid it. Let's dance."

Below the dining room, sand-blown-stone steps meandered through a grove of coconut palms to the ocean. Halfway down, where the hillside dropped sharply, a railed wooden deck jutted out on pilings. When Nicole and Grant arrived there, the tables along the edge, nearest the open-air thatched-roof bar, were filling up. In the center of the floor a dozen couples danced to a slow drum-and-guitar calypso, played by four shadowy figures in flowered shirts. A sighing darkness wrapped the scene on all sides save above, where hung the spangled canopy of the Milky Way.

"Should we find a table?" she asked.

"I don't see why." He pulled her among the dancers and gathered her to him.

And then for a long time, as the music widened its influence to the shaking floor, the trees, the wind, and the pulsating stars, they simply moved together, letting the closeness of their bodies melt all the barriers speech had thrown up. Robert and Barry and a woman named Risa: None of them had any substance compared to the heat of his hands on her waist, the solidity of his shoulder under her cheek, the sheer bulk of him in the circle of her arms. Touching, they were strangers no more. And if his tomorrow belonged to someone else, at least tonight she was not alone. This was happiness, she thought, glad she had not forgotten how to be happy.

The music grew wilder, sweeter. In the increasing crush of dancers, they spun to the dark center of the deck, where the torchlight did not penetrate.

"Enjoying yourself?" he asked with laughing exuberance as they swung around.

"Yes!" She threw her head back. "I was just wondering why I don't do this more often!"

"If I were going to be around, you would."

"But since you're not—" She danced away and back to him.

"—we'll make the most of tonight," he said, and lifted her arms around his neck.

She tightened her embrace and they became one fluid motion. "We're very good at this," she told him. "We move as if we're one person."

"But there's a better way of achieving that," he said, his hands moving down, coaxing her against him in the loud, frenzied darkness, where nobody saw or cared. The rhythms of the island poured over them like a thick syrup of rum and flowers and body-warmed perfume. All around them skirts swirled, tanned legs tossed, smiles flashed like firecrackers. And underneath everything, sweeping away yesterday and tomorrow, boomed the restless ocean.

On and on they danced. Sometimes he sang the words in her ear and sometimes she led him through a step she had learned years before, when she had first come to the islands, until the band announced the last dance before a break. Then as they were dancing the very end of that last dance, he bent her backward, in an unashamedly romantic flourish, himself hanging over her, motionless, like a hawk steadying itself for the plunge toward its prey. Looking up into his dark, brilliant gaze, Nicole felt herself opening to him and saw him recognize her desire for him. She could not believe that soon he would be gone, that this feeling would be just a half-remembered grace note on the lullaby of her life. No, it couldn't be, she couldn't let it be...

Applause greeted the end of the music. He set her upright. A couple leaving the dance floor jostled her.

With a reluctance that was like dying she shook off the intoxication.

"Thank you, sir. Very entertaining."

"Entertaining?" He pulled her into the hollow of his shoulder. "I don't concern myself with mere entertainment. Can't you see I'm seducing you?"

From a group of people at a nearby table, a woman called out to him. "Hello, there! I left a message at the desk for you. Ten o'clock tomorrow morning will be fine."

"Good enough." He nodded, and the woman, a sleek and thirtyish Harlow-type blonde, fluttered her fingers at him and went back to an interrupted conversation.

"Business?" Nicole could not keep from asking.

"Yes."

All right, she told herself, maybe it was. But the woman was still a reminder of how quickly Grant made contacts in a new place. She slid out from under his arm.

Yet they remained invisibly linked. Wordlessly, they left the deck and descended the steps to the beach. At the bottom, Nicole slipped off her shoes. They angled across the sand and turned north at the water's edge. Gradually, as blast after blast of sea air lifted her hair and whipped her skirt around her knees, the desire clouding her brain thinned. But she knew she could not dismiss what she had just experienced with him. She had never responded so quickly to any man. It frightened her, this raw attraction between them.

"Will you ever leave here? Go back to the States?" he asked, as if he too were coming back to earth.

"There's no reason to leave. The only family I have is a sister in Oregon. Besides"—arms outstretched, she revolved in a complete circle—"this is paradise. Nobody ever leaves paradise willingly."

They walked on, Grant with his hands in his pockets and his chin sunken on his chest.

"And what about you?" she inquired. "Isn't there any

place in the world that can hold you?"

"I have a piece of land back in North Carolina, with an old hunting cabin on it. I go there to relax sometimes, but if I sold it tomorrow I wouldn't miss it."

"You never shared it with anyone who meant anything to you."

His profile was suddenly sharp and hard against the sky. "You're right. How did you know that?" He sounded almost angry.

She thought about her beach cottage. "I knew."

"Let's sit down here."

To their left, a smooth shelf of rocks edged the beach for several yards. When they sat down, Nicole felt the lingering warmth of the sun in them. The beach was deserted.

Grant sat forward, loose-jointed, elbows on knees. Watching the creaming surf with him, Nicole again sensed a bond between them.

"I'm glad you didn't give up on me. I've enjoyed being with you tonight," she said.

"Well," he drawled, "I never tamed a butterfly before, so I wasn't sure how to do it. But I figured that if a person stayed very still and didn't do anything to alarm the critter, she might get used to him being around." He glanced at her. "How have I done so far?"

"You mean at the office? I guess I deserved it, but you didn't have to be *that* distant."

He lounged back on one elbow and looked up at the stars. "The problem is, I'm tired of sitting still and letting you flutter around me." He looked straight at her and dropped the joking tone. "You have a great capacity for enjoyment, Nicole. It gives you a glow that I can see right now." He caught her arm and gently pulled her nearer. "How do I share that with you? How do I reach you?"

She was leaning over him now, supporting herself on one hand, as he half reclined against the rocks. At his touch, the flames that she had been smothering since the first moment she saw him roared to life. Bending lower, so that her hair swung forward around his face, she said, "Like this," and kissed him full on the mouth.

At once his arms were around her, pulling her down on him. His lips, warm and searching, absorbed her own kiss in a longer, more passionate one, and she melted against him, riding the rise and fall of his chest. A moist vermilion mist surged in her bones, and where his heart beat against her breast, her skin sang.

After a time he took her face in his hands and held her away from him. "Do you know what this week has been like, wanting you more every minute, talking to you about cost efficiency when I wanted to be with you like this?" He eased her further over him and kissed the hollow of her throat.

"Yes, I know. I felt it too, but I blocked it out. Until now."

His hands slid down her hips, squeezing the ripe curves appreciatively and fitting themselves to her buttocks. "You drive me crazy."

"I want to drive you crazy," she heard herself say, meaning it. She feathered his face with kisses as the fever in her grew with every stroke of his hands.

With a great surge he rolled over, so that she was lying on the warm rock, her legs tangled in his, and both of them laughing. Her head fell back, her back arched like a kitten's, and in the low neck of her blouse, his mustache brushed the upper swells of her breasts. As he kissed the cleft between them, her nipples tingled.

"Let's go away for the weekend," he said, his lips returning to hers, hotter and fuller than before.

"Where?"

"Anywhere. Another island. Another country." He kissed between her breasts again and her nipples peaked higher.

"But this is so sudden." She giggled at the triteness.

"I know. But we're ready. You know that."

Why not? she asked herself, as she met his increasingly demanding kisses with a wild energy of her own. How sweet to let him break over and in her like the ocean, how satisfying to be tossed and turned by his seething drive to possess her. And in a whole weekend it would happen over and over and over, and it had been so long...

Through the climbing ecstasy, a thought struck like a lightning bolt. *She could not remember Barry's face.*

Grant must have felt her body go slack. "What is it?"

"I can't...I can't..." Struggling to sit up, she wrapped her arms about herself and screwed her eyes shut. Concentrate on a picture—the one on the wall, the ones in the albums. Memories were all she had. If she lost them, who would she be? Her mind was bare. Try to see the way he looked when he was shaving, or—

Grant kissed her lightly on the nose. "I'm sorry. I got carried away. You do that to me." Grasping her elbows, he coaxed her to her feet. "This isn't the right place."

"No." Try, try to remember!

"It's too late to get a plane out tonight, but we'll decide on that first thing in the morning. In the meantime—" his tone was playful yet tense "—your place or mine?"

"I want to go home. Alone."

The ocean sighed.

"What did you say?"

Far down the beach the silhouette of an embracing couple cut into the starry edge of the surf. With a kind of sick disgust, Nicole heard herself say, "I didn't mean to lead you on. I apologize."

He towered before her, legs apart, a wind-battered colossus. "Lady, I know when somebody comes on to me. That was not unintentional."

"But it was...wrong."

"I'd say everything was right, so far. Does that scare you? Didn't it ever feel that right before?"

Part of her knew that he was trying to understand, knew that he deserved better than this. But the rest of her was too confused to help either of them. She couldn't tell him about forgetting Barry. That was too private. Instead, she brought up the obvious objection, the one she had been ready to cast to the winds only moments before.

"Of course I'm attracted to you. But what would a weekend of sex mean to either of us? Nothing. You can go on your merry way and not mind that. I can't. It's just the way I am."

He pushed a blowing strand of hair out of her eyes. "Pleasure doesn't have to *mean* anything. Pleasure is its own excuse for being. Besides, who knows what this weekend might lead to? I can't discover everything I want to know about you in a couple of days. That much is already clear."

Nicole picked up her shoes and started walking back toward the party. "But a weekend is all there is."

"One thing at a time," he said at her shoulder. "We have to start something before we can finish it."

If this were happening with another man, would she be so confused, she wondered as they stalked along. No, it wasn't the situation, but Grant himself who made it so difficult for her to know her own mind. He already meant something to her.

The silence between them grew denser and more hopeless. The wind off the sea was colder now, and the stars were as flat as chips of ice. He had a perfect right to be angry. All night she had been swinging between reserve and seductiveness. She, who always knew exactly what she was doing and why.

They came to the steps.

"What aren't you telling me?" he demanded behind her.

She started to climb. The dancing had started again.

"It's Gresham after all, then?" His voice was low, but

so concentrated with fury that it cut through the party noise like a knife.

There were more steps than she remembered. When her calves started to cramp, she whirled on him. Because she stood on a higher step, their eyes were level.

"No, it isn't. And please don't ever bring him up again."

"Again? You think there's going to be a next time?"

Tears of embarrassment stung her eyes. "I'm sorry, I'm sorry. I can't explain. It's my fault and not yours." She turned to go, but he stopped her with a hand on her arm.

"Wait a minute." His eyes narrowed. "You're still playing the faithful wife, aren't you? Good Lord. That's it, isn't it?"

"It doesn't matter now."

"Yes, it does. Don't you realize what you're doing to yourself?"

"I don't want to talk about it." Again she turned away and again he pulled her back.

"But that's precisely what you need to do. Come up to my room. You talk and I'll listen, for as long as it takes." His thumb stroked the inside of her elbow.

"Your room?"

"Just to talk." It sounded too earnest.

"Oh, sure. And then what? Let me guess. You're going to donate your body to the Save-Nicole-From-Herself Foundation. Poor little Nicole must be starved for sex. You'll be doing her a favor. What a noble sacrifice!"

"What I'd rather give you is a good spanking."

She shook him off and fled up the steps. At the edge of the hotel lawn he caught up with her. She sped up, almost to a run, but without half trying, his long legs kept pace with her. They passed a blur of staring faces. What would the hotel gossips have to say tomorrow morning about Mrs. Starr's evening out?

On the drive in front of the hotel, she slowed to a fast walk. "Don't think you can convince me—"

"Taxi!" he roared.

A green station wagon materialized beside them. Grant jerked open the door, the cords of his neck standing out. When she had scrambled in, he slammed the door and bent to glare in her window.

"If you get over Barry any time soon, give me a call. We could have been more than lovers, you know. We could have been friends."

She had a flash of Barry, the way he used to laugh. The taxi lurched away.

CHAPTER FOUR

"HI. DO YOU KNOW where Grant is?"

Amy looked up from her typing. "Hi, Nicole. And where have you been this fine Monday morning?"

The wall clock said nine thirty-seven.

"I had to clear that shipment of supplies through Customs." Lacing and unlacing her fingers, Nicole wandered into the reception area. "Has he been in this morning?"

"He was leaving just as I got here." Amy took a rattail comb out of a desk drawer and began to fluff out her hair with the tail of it. "Robert called from Miami."

Nicole sidled to the window and scanned the distant road. "What did he want?"

"To talk to you. He sounded funny."

"Did he say where he was going?" She tapped the flat of her pencil against her palm. Nothing moved on the road.

"Where was who going?"

"Amy!" Nicole wheeled.

"Oh, *him*. Grant the Great." Amy put the comb away. "Sit down and tell Aunt Amy all about it. What's going on between you two?"

"Nothing, thanks to me." Nicole sank into the captain's chair in front of Amy's desk. "What's with the sarcasm? Don't you like him?"

"I guess so." Amy wrinkled her nose daintily. "Maybe my pride is hurt. Last week I tried every way I knew to get that man interested in me, but all he did was treat me like a little sister. And he's a slave driver in the office." She held up a thick folder. "Look what has to be typed up by this afternoon."

Nicole spread her fingers on her knees and studied her nails. "Then you're not interested in him? Personally?"

"Oh heavens, no." Amy reached for her coffee cup. Tilting back in her chair, she prepared to indulge in her second-favorite pastime: talking about men. *Doing* something about them was her favorite pastime. "Of course I went after him when he first arrived. It's kind of automatic with me, you know. And he *is* a prize. But Grant is not really my type. He's too overwhelming, too much of a heavyweight in the character department."

"Aren't you protesting too much?"

"No," Amy said a little too emphatically. "I prefer guys who aren't that strong, or that deep."

"So you can control the situation."

Amy laughed prettily at the ceiling. "Oh, Nicole, you know me too well. Now take for instance Topper Westerman. Do you remember him? The one from Los Angeles who—"

"Look, could you just tell me where I can find Grant?"

Amy sat up and gaped at Nicole. "Don't tell me. Not you. Not him."

"Why not me?"

Amy shrugged. "Well, I guess I just don't think of you in terms of men. Look at all the blind dates I've arranged for you, which you've turned down."

"This is different."

"Hmmm." Amy sipped coffee. "In a way, I guess it's wonderful. You know how much I want you to get back in circulation. But on the other hand, circulating with Grant Sutton is doing it the hard way. He's such a mysterious character. And he'll be leaving soon. It's a waste of time to make an emotional investment in him."

"You're telling me to say good-bye, when I'm trying to learn how to say hello again?"

Amy's eyes narrowed with worry. "You're not in love with him, are you?"

Nicole thought a moment. "I don't see how. There hasn't been time for that to develop. But I feel something I'm not used to feeling." She sat forward. "We had dinner together Friday night. It was perfect, until I ruined everything. But Grant said some things that have stuck with me. I've been thinking about them all weekend. He's made me take a good look at myself and do some re-evaluating. I want to tell him, Amy. That's why I have to see him."

"And here I thought you were nervous about the fashion show."

"What fashion show?"

Amy looked at her strangely. "Just what planet have you been on?"

"I've been at my beach cottage all weekend. Thinking."

"Oh boy." Amy slapped a palm to her forehead. "Then let me fill you in. Saturday afternoon, Grant was supposed to go on a picnic with me to Shell Cay. On Saturday morning he called to say he couldn't make it because he would be working here all weekend. Naturally, I assumed you would be working with him. So when I got to the office this morning and he handed me his report to type—"

"He's finished his report?"

"Almost. Apparently he decided to cut his stay short. He's finishing the rest somewhere else."

Nicole's shoulders sagged. It was too late.

"Anyway," Amy resumed, "I thought you knew he was leaving sooner than planned. That's why I've been counseling you to forget him. And I also thought you knew about the fashion show he's arranged for us to give at noon today—"

"What?" Nicole was on her feet.

"—for a group from Columbus Tours. At Fort Duncastle. In fact, that's probably where Grant is, seeing about the runway."

"But we can't." Nicole started pacing. "They do shows at the Palm Beach boutique, but we've never done one here. With the gift shop and the tours of the studio, it hasn't been necessary. We have no models, no commentary. Did you tell him that?"

"I told him."

"And what did he say?"

"I believe his exact words were, 'I'm sure the efficient Mrs. Starr is equal to the challenge.'"

Blood pounded in Nicole's temples. "If this is his idea of a joke..." Their parting on Friday evening replayed itself in her mind at double speed. No, he would not be in a joking mood. Not even now.

"He left a memo about the whole thing on your desk. Here's a copy."

Nicole caught up the paper without breaking stride. "Not bad," she mumbled grudgingly as she read. "They end up at the fort after a morning of sightseeing... umbrella tables set up around the battlements... lunch catered by the Palm Court Hotel...musicians from the Yellowbird Lounge...fashions by Seawinds..." She stopped in front of Amy. "Still, he had no right to set this up on his own."

"But we can't call it off. Columbus Tours is a big operation."

Thinking hard, Nicole folded the memo in quarters. "Get Marie Charles on the phone. The pictures of her in the brochure are good. She could model for us."

"Okay, but who else? There's not a person on this island who's had any runway experience."

"No." A smile nudged up the corners of Nicole's lips. "But I can think of two women who just might be crazy enough to try. Welcome to show business, Amy."

The next two hours were a nightmarish blur of activity. But somehow, as the bell in the ancient dockside church tolled a quarter past noon, Nicole and Amy pulled into the parking lot at the base of the fort.

"There are Marie and Dolores." Amy waved to the two young black women standing just inside the gift shop that occupied the old guardroom. "I'll take these things on ahead and explain the routine to them. See you upstairs."

Nicole made the unloading of the station wagon last as long as possible. A whimsical sea breeze made the high ground around Fort Duncastle the coolest spot on the island at that time of day. Below, the dusty, white streets of Crescent Harbour were empty and all the shops were shuttered, save for a snack stand exuding a haze of oily smoke and the aroma of fried fish. Sunlight skipped across the harbor waters like a laughing child. On the horizon basked the green mass of Turtle Cay.

A flurry of laughter caused Nicole to look up. The table umbrellas along the ramparts stood out against the cloudless sky like battle flags. People were waiting up there for her. He was up there.

With a bulging shopping bag in one hand and a bundle of clothes over her other arm, she found the claustrophobic spiral stairs that connected all levels of the fort. In the close column of air she was soon breathing hard, which didn't help her stage fright. She tried to think about something else. It wasn't like Amy to be so careful with her feelings, Nicole mused as she toiled upward.

True, Amy had never been really serious about a man in her life, not even her fiancés. But also true, Grant was a once-in-a-lifetime kind of man. Was Amy backing off from him precisely because she did feel something? And was she keeping quiet about it for Nicole's sake? Nicole halted in the doorway leading to the ramparts. It was appalling how suspicious of people's motives she had become lately. For the briefest instant, she wished Grant had never come to Silver Cay; but she didn't even try to hold onto this feeling.

The heavily female crowd from Columbus Tours was in a festive mood. The ubiquitous rum punch was flowing and box lunches were being passed out by white-shirted waiters. A low runway bisected the scattering of shaded tables and disappeared into a sort of tent made of batik panels, obviously the dressing room for the models. Every design used in the wall hangings, which were a Seawinds sideline, was represented. In the intense sunlight the colors had a hard-edged brilliance that made one's mouth water. Grant's idea, no doubt, and a good one. Movement behind the panels told her that Amy, Marie, and Dolores were getting set up. She started toward them.

From out of nowhere Grant stepped in front of her. He was wearing a red and white Seawinds sport shirt and the white duck slacks that were the recommended accompaniment to the shirt.

Nicole's throat tightened. "Hello."

"Need any help with that stuff?" His eyes were hooded, his tone strictly business.

She set the shopping bag down, flexed her fingers, and picked it up again. "No, I'm fine."

He jerked his head toward the tent. "Your people know what to do?"

"The memo was very clear." Recoiling from his coldness, her eyes fastened on a fat woman wearing a straw hat in the shape of a fruit basket loaded down with artificial fruit and a stuffed parakeet. Even Chiquita Banana wouldn't have had the nerve . . . Nicole forced herself to look at him again and said in a rush, "Grant, I have to talk to you, but not here. Please, I—"

A patch of white moved at the edge of her vision. She turned to see the Harlow blonde looking as if she been there from the beginning.

"Cynthia," Grant said, "this is Nicole Starr. Cynthia Walker."

Cynthia Walker held out a hand, then pulled it back with an apologetic laugh as she noticed Nicole's burdened arms. "I run Columbus Tours. Silver Cay is a new stop in our Sandpiper tour package. We'd like to make the Fort Duncastle fashion show a regular event, if everybody likes it."

"We'll do our best," Nicole said, feeling servile.

Cynthia turned to Grant. "You and I can work out the details any time after the show. Say around four thirty? Over drinks?"

"Excuse me," Nicole said in her sweetest voice, "but Mr. Sutton is only temporarily employed at Seawinds. Just temporary help, you know."

Cynthia Walker's penciled eyebrows jumped for her hairline.

"However," Nicole continued, "I'll be happy to discuss a permanent arrangement with you after the show. Now if you'll excuse me . . ."

When she reached the dressing room, she was shaking. "Of all the arrogance! You'd think he was chairman of the board!" she fumed to Amy.

Peering between the panels, Dolores announced, "The lunches are all served."

"Then go ahead," Nicole directed, struggling out of her clothes. Pulling on the turquoise tube dress with the fern motif, she took over the lookout post. Grant and Cynthia Walker shared a table near the end of the runway with three other people.

Conversation subsided as Dolores made her way to

the microphone and the four-piece band segued into
"Lemon Tree." The introductory remarks about Seawinds, which Nicole had finished writing less than an
hour before, began to roll out in Dolores's fine speaking
voice. Since Dolores conducted tours of Seawinds, Nicole had anticipated that she would be a good fashion
commentator.

"Now." Nicole nodded to Marie.

A murmur swept the crowd as Marie took the simple
skirt and blouse combination down the runway. Tall and
wraithlike, with liquid, almond eyes and close-cropped
curly hair, Marie was a natural clotheshorse.

Grant, sitting slouched on the base of his spine, nodded approvingly.

"How do I look?" Amy whispered, twirling in the
chocolate and white caftan.

"Great. Get ready. Here comes Marie."

Amy gave her a quick hug. "Good luck." She bounced
out, moving to the music.

Through the slit in the panels, Nicole saw Grant's face
crinkle with amusement, but he wasn't surprised. Amy,
who had never done any modeling and who was too short
to dramatize the dress, made up for both with her una-
bashed enjoyment at being the center of attention. She
took her time, working the crowd with smiles and winks.
But all too soon she was on her way back. Nicole's
stomach muscles clenched.

"It's fun, it really is," Amy bubbled, giving Nicole a
shove as she whisked past.

The sun nearly blinded her. The faces were so many
balloons on sticks. Feeling like Pinocchio trying out his
wooden joints for the first time, she moved forward, the
runway burning the soles of her bare feet. Dimly she was
aware that Dolores was describing the dress and that the
band was playing "Mary Ann." She smiled, wondering
whether she should have put Vaseline on her teeth to

make it easier. Light but steady applause reached out to her. She smiled again and the end of the runway arrived suddenly. Heart thudding, she revolved, willing herself to go slowly and to make occasional eye contact with anybody but Grant. Before she knew it, she was on her way back: and Amy and Marie were waving encouragement.

"I did it!" she exulted as the curtains closed after her. Reaching for the one-piece playsuit she would wear next, she put her eye to the peephole. Grant was sitting up straight, staring toward the tent.

Amy backed up to Nicole. "Zip this, please. He nearly fell out of his chair."

"I wish he had." But she was too elated to feel very spiteful. She decided to stop worrying about Amy; there was no envy in Amy's voice.

The next time out was easier. By her third appearance, wearing shorts and a halter top, she felt confident enough to stop short of the end, in front of Grant and Cynthia Walker. As she turned to show how the design had been centered on both pieces of clothing, she looked at him for the first time.

Beautiful, he mouthed, and gave her a thumbs-up sign. His expression was one of quizzical admiration. She didn't remember walking back up the runway.

The rest of the short program flew by. When she, Amy, and Marie went out for the last time, together, modeling three different colors of the hostess gown that was Seawinds's most popular item, Nicole was almost sorry it was over. The applause was expansive as Dolores wound up her remarks and they all moved off, waving to the crowd.

That was when the idea hit Nicole, as she looked back toward Grant, who was smugly clapping as if he deserved all the credit for their performances.

Nicole walked back to the midpoint of the runway.

"Ladies and gentlemen, that concludes our showing of women's fashions. But we haven't forgotten the well-dressed man."

He didn't see it coming, not even when she stepped off the runway in front of him and took his arm.

"What the hell—?"

"The gentleman is a little shy. Let's give him some encouragement!"

Applause and whistles. Was it planned? Did they know each other? Nicole could sense people wondering.

The band started up again, shaking the air with a hot goombay beat.

Tugging on him, smiling fixedly at the crowd, she got him on the runway. Grant glared around him like a freshly caught grizzly bear.

"Seven hundred islands in the Bahamas and I had to land on this one," he growled out of the side of his mouth.

"Grant is wearing our popular beachcomber shirt and white duck pants," Nicole said cheerily. "Both come in sizes small, medium, large, and extra large." Under her breath she said, "Smile. It's good for business."

He bared his teeth.

A man sitting near the runway was wearing a new straw hat. Nicole motioned to him and he good-naturedly handed it up to her.

"In our gift shop," she shouted over the music, "you can find straw planter's hats made right here in Crescent Harbour, with batik bands to match our shirts." She set the hat on Grant's head and adjusted the brim. There was murder in his eyes.

"You knew I didn't have any models," she accused him *sotto voce*. "You knew I'd have to get up here myself."

"I didn't. But you did fine. So what's the problem?"

"Would you mind turning around to show the back of the shirt?"

Grant turned in a circle, with more poise than Nicole

wanted him to possess. He flashed a smile and winked at the woman in the fruit basket hat. She stifled an ecstatic squeal behind a chubby fist.

"No problem," Nicole resumed the conversation when he was facing her again. "But a general oughtn't to order his troops to do anything he wouldn't do himself. I thought you deserved a turn on the runway, too."

"You mean I get to be a general? I'd expect to be a buck private in this woman's army."

"Please unbutton your shirt."

"Oh. I see." Grant started unbuttoning and was rewarded with a chorus of wolf whistles. "I'm a one-star general and you're a five-star."

To the crowd Nicole said, "The shirt can be worn outside or in. Tied at the waist"—she began to tie it—"it is the perfect companion to swimming trunks. Also note that the slacks have a drawstring waist, for maximum coolness and comfort."

"Have you changed, or did I meet your serious twin last week?" he whispered.

"I've changed. That's what I want to talk to you about." She undid her shell necklace and informed their audience, "The heavier shell necklaces, also made here, such as this one of tortoise and puka shell, can be worn by men as well as women. Since the materials come from the sea, you can wear them when you go swimming without damaging them." To fasten the necklace on Grant, she stepped in close and raised her arms around his neck.

Instantly she was captured in his arms. He grinned down at her.

Nicole twisted half away from him and tried to resume, "And for a quiet evening at home, or perhaps for an après-swim dinner around the pool, there's our short kimono wrap of the same mater—" To Grant she hissed, "I can hardly breathe. Stop it."

"Are you kidding?" He chuckled through his public smile. Keeping her pinned against him with one arm, he tipped his hat to the crowd, then settled it rakishly over one eye. "Dance," he ordered and began to move her around. The band was on its theme song, "Yellow Bird."

"But I haven't finished—"

"Or do I have to carry you?" He pushed her backward, more or less in rhythm, toward the dressing room. The crowd, sensing the struggle, buzzed and tittered.

"This isn't dancing. It's being run over by a bulldozer." Over his shoulder she called, "Please visit our gift shop, located in the historic Seawinds Plantation on Castleton Road, to see our full line of menswear. Our models will be passing among you now with brochures and a free sachet of tropical herbs and flowers sealed in an envelope of Seawinds batik. Tours of our workshop leave every morning from—"

Grant turned and skimmed the hat back to its owner. As he pushed her into the tent, the applause was chaotic.

The tent was empty.

He didn't let her go. "Didn't know what you might ask me to do next," he remarked sardonically.

"You would have deserved it. Grant, you had no right to commit us to this show without telling me."

"If you had come to the office over the weekend like you were supposed to, you would have known about it."

"Well, excu-uuse me. I thought *I* was running Seawinds."

"It was running you. You weren't looking beyond the details."

"I don't agree," Nicole argued, "but anyway, that's not the point. You infringed on my authority." His bare chest distracted her momentarily. With an effort, she gathered her wits to say, "If I were a man, you wouldn't have dared."

"If you were a man. What a dull thought." He folded her closer.

"See what I mean?"

"Look," he said with a hint of annoyance, "I didn't

have a month to think this over. The tour group is leaving tonight. I did you a big favor. Getting this show established with Columbus Tours is going to mean a lot more business for you."

"Oh, really? And just what kind of business deal *did* you strike with Cynthia Walker? What was your half of the bargain?"

"Now who's being sexist? I told you on Friday night that I had business to discuss with her."

"Then you could have told me what it was about. Whatever concerns Seawinds concerns me."

"We weren't dealing with business then, remember? Because you *are* a woman, we had other things in mind. At least until—" He let her go and ran a hand through his hair. "I didn't want to end fighting this way, Nicole." He looked past her.

Things fell together inside her. She turned away, saw clothes that needed picking up, and started doing it. "When are you leaving?"

"Within the hour."

"I see." She went on fooling with the clothes. It was suffocating inside the tent. The talk and music outside seemed much farther away than they were.

"Something came up with one of my clients," he said to her back. "They're sending a company plane. You'll get my report later in the week."

The dress she was trying to put on a hanger kept slipping off. It occurred to her that he had known about his change of plans for some time. That was why he had worked all weekend to wrap up the Seawinds investigation. That was why he had been so intent on getting her into bed Friday night. It was then or never.

"I'm not interested in the report," she said savagely. "I'm going to go on running things exactly as I have been." It wasn't true. She did care.

"So I was paid to conduct an exercise in futility?"

"It wasn't my money."

He spun her around. Instinctively, she held up the dress for protection. He whipped it out of her hands and threw it on the floor. Nicole searched his face, wondering what she was looking for. She didn't find it.

"You are the most infuriating woman," he ground out. His fingers tightened on her arms. "And yet—"

"Hello! Anybody home?" Cynthia Walker pushed wide one side of the tent and marched in, trailed by several well-upholstered ladies. "Grant, dear, I have some people here who want to meet you. You're a star! Oh hello, Nicole. You too, of course. I hope we're not interrupting anything?"

"Not at all." Her eyes still locked with his, Nicole pried Grant's fingers loose from her arms. "Good-bye, Grant."

He grinned suddenly, the ladies' man who never quite gives up on a prospect. "Look, who knows, maybe some-day—"

"No. I don't think so."

The ladies surrounded them, chattering among themselves.

Chin up, voice steady, Nicole said to him, "When your face is on the cover of *GQ*, don't forget who gave you your big chance."

As she hurried away, she heard one of the women ask Grant, "Haven't I seen you in one of those beer commercials on TV? 'You only go around once' or something?"

Pushing her way through the tables and milling tourists, Nicole spotted a wiry, half-good-looking man dressed in khaki surveying the crowd from a doorway. He was palming a cigarette and undressing the better-built women with his eyes, with a rapid ease that made Nicole think of peeling a banana. He was typical of his breed, as Barry had been. She could always tell a pilot.

She walked over to him. "You must be looking for Mr. Sutton. He's over there."

The pilot undressed her, too, with his eyes. "Thanks." He drifted.

"Nicole!" Amy came scurrying up. "I have never been so surprised in my life!"

"At what?"

"At you. You really must have changed. Getting Grant up on that runway was so bold!"

"Thanks. I surprised myself."

"How did it go afterward?" Amy winked broadly. "In the tent, I mean."

"Oh," Nicole replied offhandedly, while a little knife sawed away inside, "I gave it my best shot all right, but the target's leaving town. Would you girls mind cleaning up here? I'll see you in a little while."

Half an hour later, when she had walked around the island as far as Devil's Cove, a Brittan Trilander took off in the direction of Nassau. Nicole waded out in the water, up to her thighs, and watched it until it disappeared.

CHAPTER FIVE

LIKE A FLEET of Spanish galleons the towering thunder-heads came on, filling the sky. Nicole, doing a lazy backstroke, watched them conquer the sun. The sea was glassy, the air heavy and calm. It was a Sunday made for solitude.

With a yawn, she rolled over and paddled ashore. As she stretched out face down on her towel, the sun burst through again. She gave herself up to its skillful massage. She knew her lethargy was the result of her late night out with Amy and the two businessmen. It had been more fun than she had expected, but less entertaining than the worst moment she had ever had with Grant. At least she had made a start. She was back in circulation again, which pleased her somewhat and pleased Amy greatly, and she was beginning to forget Grant. It had been almost three weeks now since he'd gone out of her life. Two weeks, six days, two hours and . . . hell. She'd never forget.

She turned on her back and took down the straps of her bathing suit. Things were back to normal, or as normal as they were ever going to get. Robert was arriving the following Thursday to see about the changes she'd made at Seawinds, as recommended in Grant's report. Tomorrow she would get busy painting the cottage. She dozed, slipping in and out of sleep with the shift of the clouds over the sun. A boat buzzed somewhere. She almost dreamed.

The noise of the boat got louder. From the roughness of the motor, she could tell that it was one of the rental boats. It was coming her way, probably heading for Garden Reef with a load of weekend divers. She dozed off again.

The sound of a hull scraping bottom snapped her awake. She sat up.

"This is a private b—"

He waded ashore, carrying the old brown loafers in one hand and a florist's box in the other.

Nicole scrambled to her feet, holding up the top of her suit.

His mustache, longer than she remembered, framed an indolent grin. Compared to the meltdown in his eyes, the sun was nothing.

He stopped in front of her. "You said you wanted to talk."

They both moved at the same time. The shoes hit the sand to one side of her, the florist's box to the other. She leaped into his arms.

"I never thought I'd see you again!" Laughing, not caring that he would know now how much she cared, she hung on as he swung her around. When he set her back on her feet, she peered up at him incredulously, shading her eyes. "But why? Why did you come back?"

"Had to." He rested his forearms on her shoulders in a heavy, friendly way. "Just had to."

"Me and my smart mouth. You probably came back to get the last word."

"Maybe. All I know is I'd rather fight with you than do anything else with any other ten women I know."

"Is that ten all at once, or one at a time?"

"This is how I handle smart mouths." He kissed her long and hard, until it seemed that every tingling inch of her body was being touched by his lips. She began to writhe delicately against him, feeling, although he was not moving, a rhythm building between them.

"Any more remarks?" he asked.

"Yes. Do it again."

After a while he let her go and scooped up the florist's box. "Brought you a present."

She tied up her straps, then tore into the box like a greedy child. "Irises! I haven't seen an iris in years! We don't have them here."

"There wasn't much point in bringing hibiscus."

"But at this time of year, how did you find them anywhere?"

"I found them." He looked off, uncomfortable at having been caught going to so much trouble. "That's your house?"

"Yes, I'll show it to you."

But at the porch, her heart quailed. What would she do with him inside? The cottage was as small as a doll's house, with no room to keep her distance from him. Then, as he crossed the threshold to her private world, she experienced a subtly satisfying sense of violation. After that, distance was the last thing on her mind.

In the kitchen, she ran water in a vase and jumbled the iris stalks in attractively. Grant prowled the living room, looking as out of place as a lion at a garden party amidst her spindly white furniture. He examined the silk-screened prints of sea creatures on the walls. He glanced over the small bookcase, touching the backs of the Emily

Dickinson and the Edna St. Vincent Millay poetry volumes as if he had expected to find them there. He saw it all: the needlepointed pillows that her mother had done, the guitar, the framed Portuguese saying, *É tão facil ser feliz*, it is so easy to be happy, which she wished she believed.

As she came into the room with the tray of drinks she had prepared, he turned and studied her with the same attention. She tensed, wondering why he had really come back. The short answer, she realized immediately, was in the way he was looking at her legs.

"I made lime rickeys. It's so hot," she said unnecessarily. His presence made the air denser. She imagined a cloudburst brewing just below the ceiling. Handing him a glass, she attempted a teasing tone. "Just make yourself at home while I slip into something less comfortable."

"Don't bother on my account." He downed half the drink in one swallow. His eyes, heavy lidded, smoldered lazily.

Setting the tray down, Nicole fled to the bedroom and shut the door behind her. For a moment she leaned against it, wanting to lock it but not wanting him to hear the click. Then she stripped off her suit and hopped out of it on the way to the adjoining bath, where she quickly showered off salt and sand. When she was pulling on her dress, she heard papers rustling. By the time she opened the door, spray cologne still tingling on the backs of her knees, he was settled on the sofa with the morning paper, looking almost domestic.

He tossed the newspaper aside and patted the couch next to him. "Come here."

When she was beside him, legs curled under her, he handed her drink to her and draped an arm around her. "Now. Tell me what the trouble was with Barry."

She stiffened. "There wasn't—"

"Come on. If you don't work through that, then I

came back for nothing." He waited: grave, interested, somehow tender.

"It was that easy for you to see? That the problem was with the marriage and not with Barry's . . . death?"

"Yes." His palm cupped her shoulder, stroking with a circular motion.

This was what she had wanted, wasn't it? A chance to explain? But doing it was something else. She took a long drink and set the glass down. "It was a good marriage in many ways. That's what made it so hard afterward. I couldn't put the might-have-been part of it behind me, the sickening, unfinished feeling over and above the sheer loss of him . . ."

Wind blasted straight across the room, belling out the ruffled curtains on the north windows and flattening the opposite ones.

"Go on."

She took a deep breath and expelled it. "I met him through friends when I was nineteen and working in California. He was on leave from the Air Force and seemed terribly glamorous. I was away from home for the first time, pretty inexperienced, and here was this 'older man' in a unifrom who'd been to all the exotic places I'd only read about. For a year and a half I was there waiting whenever he had a leave. As soon as he was discharged, we married and moved to Florida, where he worked for Robert, piloting a company plane. After that we came here, to start Starr Charter." Grant was rubbing the nape of her neck. She laid her cheek against his chest. "It wasn't until Silver Cay that I realized I didn't really know the man I'd married. Before the wedding, we saw each other only a weekend here and there. Afterward, it was the same." She raised her head. "I was ready to tell you all this the day of the fashion show. But now it makes me uncomfortable. After all, Barry can't defend himself."

"That can't be helped. Keep going."

She snuggled into him, taking courage from his warmth and strength. "The original idea was for Barry to move into administration, as soon as we could afford it. But almost immediately he made it clear that flying—and the rootless life it entailed—was his great love. He didn't want a home. He didn't care about children. I found myself taking on more and more of the business end of Starr Charter, working fourteen-hour days while he hired himself out to wealthy island-hoppers. The wealthy ones always asked for Barry. I couldn't keep the schedules straight because sometimes he would be days late coming back. I began to suspect that he was involved in something illegal, maybe drug traffic. Sometimes I thought there was another woman. He never gave straight answers to my questions. But once there was this phone call—" She cringed and bowed her head. She had never told anybody about the doubts.

"It's all right. It's okay." He massaged the area between her shoulder blades. "Don't say anything else. It's all right."

"No." She sat up, her lashes wet. "I have to finish. The last day, we had a terrible argument. I had found out that he'd filed a false flight plan the week before. Who he wanted to deceive, besides me, I never knew. Or maybe he wanted to protect me. Anyway, I remember that we were standing on the runway, just before he took off again, and we both said things we shouldn't have. Things we would have taken back the next day. I said...I said that since he didn't want a family, didn't want the responsibility of the business, didn't want to take me into his confidence...he didn't have to come back." She strangled a sob. "He never did. Do you know what the Tongue of the Ocean is? It's a trench in the ocean floor, over a mile deep. That's where he went down. Maybe if we hadn't had that argument, maybe his judgment—"

"Stop it. You weren't responsible for the storm."

"I know. But still—" The sobs broke through and she shook against him.

His arms went around her. "But you've got to let go of it, Nicole," he said quietly. "It was over a long time ago. You're still here, with a life to live."

She was wondering if she would be able to stop crying when, abruptly, the need to do so left her. She looked up at Grant. In a shaky whisper she managed to say, "I loved him."

"I know. You wouldn't do anything less."

"And there were good times. Very good."

"There always are. That's the hell of it." He pulled her closer and kissed the crown of her head. Nicole buried her face in his chest. Gradually her ragged breathing smoothed out. She smelled rain and closed her eyes.

After a time Grant mused, "So running the charter service gave you the management skills to take over at Seawinds. I wondered where you got them." He reached for his glass, drained it, and went on. "Whatever his good points, your husband used you and used you hard. No wonder you're so sensitive about your authority at Seawinds, about Gresham imposing me on you, and then about me making executive decisions without consulting you." He kissed her hair again. "Baby, I'm sorry."

It began to rain. Time stretched out.

The tears had dried on her face like glue. She yawned. Crying always made her sleepy. So had the swim and the drink and being understood.

"It was the guilt," she murmured. "The leftover guilt about the way it ended with Barry. That's what made me run from you on the beach, I guess." She told him about forgetting Barry's face, then finished. "I've been using him as an excuse to run for so long..." She sighed and nestled closer, hugging him to her. "You made me see that." She yawned again. She felt cleansed and new.

There was more quiet time while her mind went on playing the game that she was going to sleep. But her body was lasciviously awake, thrilling to the touch of the stroking hand on her hip. Her breasts grew heavier; the swirling spot low in her abdomen, warmer and softer. She was free. It kept striking her consciousness anew: She was free and ready to use that freedom.

As if he knew what she was thinking, Grant lifted her hair and kissed the nape of her neck. "Come on."

He stood up and lifted her into his arms. She wound her arms around his neck and kissed his cheek. Then their lips met in a new, frank way that left her breathless. As he carried her into the bedroom, objects shone with a luminous clarity, as if seen through sunlit water. Rain whispered on the roof. She inhaled his clean, masculine scent and knew that after this, being a woman would take on a deeper meaning.

In the bedroom he ran his hands over her thighs and breasts as he set her down.

"God, I want you."

They came together in an open-mouthed kiss, tongues exploring in passionate haste. His hands closed over her breasts, discovering their pert roundness. As he squeezed them gently, Nicole gasped and took his lower lip in her teeth. Nuzzling his neck, she closed her eyes while he undid the buttons at her shoulders that held the terrycloth sundress on her. Then he peeled the dress down and she stepped out of it, clad only in bikini panties.

He held her out from him, by the waist, and took his time looking her over. Under his gaze, her nipples grew hard and hotly pink, begging to be kissed. She stepped up to him and took him in her arms, her near-nakedness against him. His head ducked suddenly and he sucked each nipple in turn. Convulsively her pelvis thrust against him and she felt his arousal like a branding iron. His lips came up to hers, insistent and swollen with heat. His hands touched her buttocks, then impatiently pushed inside her panties. Her body was one molten throb. She molded herself to him, like a young vine possessing an oak. If this was making love, then she had never made love before.

All at once, tearing his lips from hers, Grant caught up her right hand, stripped off her wedding ring, and tossed it on the nightstand. She stared at the white circle on her finger where it had been. Then she looked into his eyes. The fierce blaze of the conqueror lit them.

"You're mine now." Taking her by the hips, he pushed her backward onto the bed.

As she watched him undress, her body was so eager that she could not keep still. Tossing voluptuously, it anticipated the ravishment. Then he was naked: a bronzed, muscled god at her bedside. She had never wanted anything so much in her life. She held up her arms and he rolled into them, kissing her mouth, eyes, and shoulders before his lips went once more to her breasts, teasing them with excruciating care. Twining her fingers in his hair, she coaxed, "Oh now, please, now." But it was not time for that. Kissing her stomach, he removed her panties. As his hands began to explore her, awakening sleepy, intimate spots into pulsing desire, she gradually responded with a driven curiosity of her own. It was all new, as if she had never touched a man's body before. Smoothing him with kisses, she stroked and cajoled him until his breath whistled through his teeth. And just when she thought she would go crazy from the spiral of ecstasy that soared higher and higher yet never seemed to get any nearer to the top, he let himself down on her. Gripping his shoulders she tilted herself to receive him, panting, half smiling into the dark face she suddenly believed she had seen years before, in dreams of heroes. A little cry escaped her. Then there was an exquisite sliding. For an instant, they remained motionless, caught in wonder.

"My virgin."

"It is like that, almost . . . like there was never anybody else . . ."

They began to move together, like long, liquid waves

washing a sunlit shore. But slowly the rhythm built in urgency and force, until he was like the sea at night, beating against the mysterious, cloudy headland that was herself. Her nails raked his back and her teeth were bared against his shoulder, the salt taste of his skin on her tongue as the long shuddering crash unfolded, sundering her, like the sea parting, like the rock splitting, until suddenly they dissolved into one action and feeling, so that when she screamed aloud, the sound seemed to come from him.

Humming to herself, Nicole set the platter on the table and surveyed the effect—the irises in the center, flanked by candles, hot bread, bacon and eggs, a bowl of fresh fruit and a platter of cheese. Not spectacular, but not bad either, considering that she hadn't been expecting company. She went to the linen drawer for napkins. They had lain talking for hours. The rain had stopped and it was dark outside. On the radio, Frank Sinatra was singing about strangers in the night. And there was something familiar about all this. She couldn't quite put her finger on it, but the candles, the feeling of surfeit when her stomach was empty, the radio, all reminded her of something. She wasn't sure she wanted to know what it was.

The screen door opened and Grant came in from the beach. Her uneasy feeling evaporated.

"There's a full moon," he said. "Do you feel a little crazy?" His lips grazed hers.

"Yes, but it isn't the moon." She returned his kiss. "Dinner's ready."

"So is the champagne." He reached in the refrigerator for the bottle he had earlier brought in from the boat.

The cork ricocheted into a hanging fern pot and they cheered.

Nicole held the glasses while he poured. "I'd like to propose a toast to your save-me-from-myself organization. Your lifesaving techniques are something else."

He hooked a finger in the belt of her wrap and pulled her close. "You haven't seen them all yet."

The soundless sound of champagne bubbles popping filled the room for a while.

"Hey," she finally said between kisses, "dinner's getting cold."

"Okay, but just remember that my definition of 'once' is 'not enough.'"

"I'll take it under advisement." As they filled their plates, she said teasingly, "I just have one question. What are you saving me *for*?"

"To go to Nassau with me tomorrow."

She stopped buttering bread.

"I have a couple of days before I have to be in Caracas. I want to spend them with you." He grinned, "Okay? We'll do the town."

"Sounds great." She smiled. And yet, where was it all leading, besides nowhere? "Robert is coming next Thursday to go over your esteemed report. I have to be back by then."

"You will be."

A surge of the old anger swept over her. Was she just filler to him? Something to fill up the little bit of spare time he might have once in a while? Or worse, would Nassau be the end? Yet nothing in the world could stop her from going. She would travel all the way to China for ten minutes with him and consider herself lucky. On the radio, Patsy Cline was singing "Crazy." It was too appropriate.

They talked of other things as they ate, of the places they had been, of growing up, and, finally, laughing uproariously, of the fashion show. After dinner was cleared away they had coffee on the porch, listening to the waves and to the post-rain breeze talking to itself in the undergrowth behind the cottage. The lights of a ship hung on the horizon like a low constellation. After a time of being quiet together, Grant got to his feet and pulled her up with him.

"How about a moonlit dip in the ocean?"

"So soon after dinner?"

"I didn't say we were going to swim."

"Oh. I see," she said innocently as his fingers found the sash of her wrap. "Well, in that case"—the wrap slipped from her shoulders—"I'll race you to the water!"

Making love in the shallows, the waves rocking them as they rocked together, they achieved a wild sweetness unlike anything she had ever known.

It was not until after two in the morning, when Grant was sleeping heavily beside her in the bed she had never before shared, that she placed the uncomfortable feeling that had troubled her before dinner.

This was the way it had been with Barry, more times than she cared to remember: the unexpected arrival of her man after she had given up expecting him, the gifts, the lovemaking, the brave pretense that the bliss would go on forever, followed by his inevitable departure, he as charming as ever, leaving her to cope again with the loneliness. Nicole sat up and hugged her knees. She gazed at Grant's face in the moonlight. Even in repose, its sensual strength made her go weak all over. But was she falling for another Barry? She recalled a friend of her mother's who had married three alcoholics in a row. Was some flaw in her own nature drawing her to a man who could only make her unhappy? She fell back on her pillow. No, he wasn't like Barry. He wasn't. She wouldn't let herself think so. She wouldn't let him be. She rolled on her stomach and pushed the thought out of her mind. It dropped away decisively, like a grand piano going over a cliff. She slept, dreamlessly.

CHAPTER SIX

WHEN NICOLE AWOKE the next morning she was still lying on her stomach, one arm flung wide. Vaguely she remembered Grant slipping out from under it sometime before. In the bathroom, the shower was going full blast. Eyes still closed, she rolled over to his side of the bed. It was still warm. Smiling, she curled into a ball.

During her marriage to Barry, they had both come to take for granted the second pillow on the bed, the table set for two, the traces of another person's habits around the house. She supposed that all couples came to that, in time. Marriage lost its newness just as a pair of shoes did; and like the shoes, it might become more comfortable for having done so.

She opened her eyes and propped herself up on one elbow. Still, if she ever married again, things would be different. She would cherish the shared times more, because she understood now how precious those times were and how quickly they could be taken away. Of course, she would choose her partner more wisely next time . . .

The shower cut off.

Consider a man like that, she thought to herself. She could not imagine ever taking Grant for granted (smiling at the pun), no matter how many years they spent together.

With a frown, she jumped out of bed. What she needed was some hot coffee and a cold shower.

In the kitchen she measured out grounds and poured cold water into the coffee machine. By the time she had done that, her daydreams were under control. They stayed that way until she returned to the bedroom with two mugs of coffee.

The bathroom door was ajar. A moist smell of shaving cream filtered out. Nicole sat down on the edge of the bed, struck by a pain that was almost physical. The smell of shaving cream: a simple thing, but how she had missed it all these years! And how she would miss it next week, when she was again alone.

"Nicole, are you awake? We'll have to be getting to the airport soon."

"Yes. I have coffee for you." Was that it? she thought suddenly. Was she so lonely, so hungry for a man's attentions that any man would do? If that were true, then she was using Grant every bit as much as she suspected he was using her.

He came out of the bathroom in slacks, bare chested, toweling off stray dabs of shaving cream. "Mmmm, coffee smells good." He bent to kiss her.

"Grant"—she handed him his mug, then clutched her own with both hands—"I've decided to go to Nassau with you."

He set his mug on the dresser. "You just decided? I thought we settled that last night."

"I never actually said yes." She looked down at her reflection in the hot liquid.

"You could have fooled me," he said warily. He slipped into a shirt. "I must have been going by your actions. They were saying yes, loud and clear." When he had finished buttoning the shirt and she remained silent, he added, "I took it for granted—"

"We shouldn't take anything for granted between us! Not anything!"

He folded his arms and studied her for a while. "No, we shouldn't. Thanks for deciding in my favor."

"I'll be ready in a few minutes," she told him and started for the bathroom.

"Nicole."

She turned.

He took his time sipping coffee and squinting at her through the steam. Finally he said, "As long as we're not taking anything for granted, let's get the purpose of this trip straight."

Her stomach did a neat flip, up in the air and down, like a pancake. "All right."

"I enjoy your company, but you have to know where I stand. The trouble with most women, whether they admit it or not, is that they seek permanence blindly, the way a sunflower follows the sun. You impressed me as being different, from the beginning."

"Because I played hard to get?"

"A lot of women do that, to tease. You were serious about it. I liked that. I like your independence and your involvement in a career. You aren't just playing at work until a man comes along to take you away from it all."

"How can you be so sure? You seem to think all women are conniving. Why make an exception for me?" Her voice crackled thinly, like a voice on a faraway radio station.

"Because you're so transparent. I can always read your

feelings on your face." His eyes narrowed. "Or are you just a superb actress?"

"Oh no, not me. What you see is what you get," she declared brightly. "You know something? I think it's terribly arrogant of you to assume that every woman wants you for keeps. I certainly don't."

"Is that so?"

"I know a bad risk when I see one. Believe me, you are definitely a weekend fling, not a permanent arrangement. 'Bye." As she closed the bathroom door, she had a glimpse of a man who was just beginning to think he had gotten more than he bargained for.

She leaned against the wall, head down, feeling as if she had been kicked in the chest by a mule. All right, she thought, so he wanted to play the game: I want you to want me, but I don't want you. Why hadn't he said so the instant he stepped onto her beach, before everything got so beautiful and intimate? Anger built in her until she could almost see it shining through her skin. Arrogant rogue. As soon as a woman began to care for him, he walked out on her, did he? Well, two could play at that game. She nodded to herself. Yes, she would teach Grant what it felt like to care about someone who didn't care about him. She was too smart to fall in love with another Barry. Instead, she would make him fall in love with her.

While she washed her face, she studied herself in the bathroom mirror. Could she do it? Could a woman with practically no experience in romance bring a man like Grant to his knees? She shrugged at her reflection. At least she had nothing to lose. In a few days he would be gone anyway. She would play his game and win; and he would pay the penalty.

By the time she had dressed, packed, and telephoned Amy to say that she wouldn't be at work for a couple of days, she could hear the taxi approaching on the beach road. From the noise, she guessed it was Leroy, a driver who always operated with all the windows down and the radio blaring.

As they were pulling away from the cottage, Grant tucked her arm into the crook of his. "Ready for a good time?"

"Aren't we already having one?"

"A better time, then." He patted her arm. "It just keeps on getting better, doesn't it?"

"Yes, it does." For a couple more days, she wanted to taunt him, and then we'll see who's cheerful. She thought of Amy's teasing advice on the phone: "Make the most of Nassau, Nicole. You'll never get another chance like this!" She recalled something else too: a forced gaiety in Amy's voice that had rung suspiciously false. Envy rearing its head again? But it was too late now to worry about anybody but herself.

"When was the last time you were in Nassau?" Grant wanted to know.

"Oh, it's been years and years."

"Don't all commerical flights from this part of the Bahamas go through there? Or have you been traveling by ship?"

Her palms had been sweating since the arrival of the taxi. She wiped them on her skirt. "I haven't traveled that far since Barry died. I've——" she swallowed embarrassment—"been terrified of flying since then."

He stroked his mustache. "You've been subdued this morning. Is that why?"

"Yes." It was partly true, anyway.

"It couldn't be any more dangerous than this," he remarked with a chuckle. "We're practically airborne now."

The taxi was slamming around curves and barreling down straights like a berserk pinball. Leroy slapped the steering wheel in time to the radio, pretending to play bongo drums. There seemed to be very little steering going on. The song was a reggae-flavored political number urging the listener to "Get involved! Get involved!" Wryly Nicole wondered who was writing the soundtrack to her fling with Grant.

There was nothing ceremonial about air service on Silver Cay. Two minutes after stepping out of the taxi, they were buckling seatbelts. In another two, the plane was taxiing.

"How do you feel?" Grant asked.

"Frailty, thy name is airplane." A shallow pulse beat in the hollow of her throat. "To tell you the truth, I've never really believed that man can fly. Even when I'm up in the air, I have a sneaking suspicion that it's all done with mirrors."

He took her hand. "Hey, you're trembling."

"I told you." She lay back, panting. The intercom crackled instructions, but her brain didn't register them. She hoped she wouldn't faint or be sick. Drearily she wondered how she could expect to gamble her heart against Grant's and win, when she didn't even have the courage to take a plane ride.

"Anything else you're afraid of?" he asked to distract her.

"Just love and death."

"You and everybody else."

The plane bumbled around a turn, moving like a very old turtle. Nicole closed her eyes. Why had she said that about love and death? She hadn't known she was going to. Because, she answered herself, she was too scared to lie. And of the two, she was probably more afraid of love.

Rattling all over with the effort of gathering itself for the leap, the plane accelerated toward takeoff. Inside Nicole, its speed was matched by a nauseating pull as the screws of fear tightened, tightened. Her lips formed a soundless O of panic as the certainty of annihilation gripped her.

Grant took both of her hands in his. "I'm right here,

Nicole . . . hold tight . . . come on, you'll be all right . . . there's nothing to worry about . . . that's it, hold on to me. . . . There. You can open your eyes now."

She craned to look out the window. They were just clearing the reefs of Silver Cay, heading out over turquoise water. Relief, then exhilaration flooded her.

"You make me feel so alive!"

"Let's give the pilot a little credit." But he was clearly pleased.

The flight to Nassau was not long. Over the complimentary orange juice they discussed Grant's report. Though his style was, predictably, more aggressive than hers, their thinking on business practices was remarkably similar.

"But there's one thing that has puzzled me from the beginning," Nicole remarked. "Why did you concern yourself with Seawinds in the first place? It's such a small operation."

"Gresham was willing to pay my fee."

"But I've heard that you're more interested in a challenge than in money. A little batik studio is no challenge. And by the very nature of the product, it can never be mechanized and computerized into a big industry."

"You forget my background in textiles. That naturally made Seawinds more interesting to me."

As Nicole eyed him obliquely, her mind flew back to the day when Grant and Robert had arrived on Silver Cay. She'd suspected that Robert was hiding something from her. She felt the same way now with Grant. She sensed trouble ahead but didn't want to think about it. She wanted her mind clear for the current challenge.

"I'm glad you took on Seawinds, for whatever reason," she said. "If you hadn't, we never would have met."

He patted her knee and nodded, thinking of something else.

The intercom advised them that the descent to Nassau

had begun. Mixed with the apprehension at landing, Nicole felt a thrill of anticipation. For a moment she even considered abandoning her plans for emotional sabotage. All she really wanted to do was enjoy herself. She was bored by the thought of all the years she had spent being sensible and industrious, like the ant in the fable. Like the grasshopper instead, she wanted to use up all her happiness in this man's presence and think not of the lean, wintry times when he would be gone. When he took her hand, she grasped his gratefully.

"That's an improvement," Grant observed. "No nerves?"

They were on the ground.

"One flight with you and my fear of flying seems to be cured," Nicole said in surprise.

"Double meaning duly noted. Of course, we'll have to keep making test flights, just to be sure."

Inside the airport, the bustle and noise had a contagious gaiety. From the international concourse came the strains of a West Indian calypso band welcoming travelers from the States. Farther on, lines of sunburned, happily frazzled tourists jammed the ticket counters for departing flights.

"Honeymooners on their way home?" Nicole guessed, noting that most of the people were young and stood in twos.

"Little do they know what awaits them." Grant steered her through a crush of people and luggage.

"What?"

"The real world."

It was something Barry might have said. Barry, who detested permanence and serenity, who never should have committed himself to one woman...

They arrived at the baggage claim. Grant left her to retrieve the suitcases. It was too bad he wasn't another kind of man, she thought wistfully, before she could stop herself.

Outside, a few minutes later, Grant hailed a black Cadillac limousine. They were soon on the road to Nassau, with the palms along the way nodding a greeting and the sky a bright, shouting blue.

"Where to?" Nicole asked more brusquely than she meant to.

He cocked an eyebrow. "You're not going to go independent on me again, are you, and demand to approve the schedule of events in advance?"

"I'm sorry. I like having someone else make the decisions for a change. I like being taken care of. It's just that I haven't had that luxury for a long time. I'm not used to it."

"I'm not used to taking care of anybody either." Looking out the window, he mused half to himself, "But it's all right. It's okay."

They rode on in a fragile silence. Put what he had just said together with the crack about honeymooners, Nicole reflected, and the message you got was, *Stay away closer*. It pretty nearly matched her own ambivalence.

By now they were on the outskirts of Nassau, passing through an energetic mixture of garishly painted shanties, new construction, and middle-size commerical establishments: the tropics being dragged by the heels into modern times. The sidewalks were teeming; the traffic, a patient, sweating crawl of taxis, American and British cars, motorbikes, and the occasional horse-drawn carriage of tourists. There was a humming boom-town excitement in the air that made Nicole proud of her adopted country.

Farther in, they hit the part of town that she remembered. On Shirley Street they passed Government House, a squarish pink and white edifice that made her think of a large petit four. It was the official residence of the governor general of the Bahamas. During World War II, Nicole recalled, it had been home to the duke and duchess of Windsor. She was glad to see again the Royal Victoria Hotel, which, during the American Civil War, had been the center of the blockade-running business and thus a hotbed of Yankee spies and of Southern businessmen making deals for the Confederacy. Now, like a high-toned old lady fallen on hard times, it nodded among lacy greenery in the twilight of life, dreaming of unfaded grandeur.

The taxi fishtailed down a sloping side street and pulled up in front of a white stone building. The brass plate by the door read ARTHUR PICKENS INTERNATIONAL. In the display window, as a backdrop for an ebony mannequin wearing a white crocheted bikini and a gold and lapis lazuli necklace, hung one of the Seawinds wall hangings.

"Stunning effect," Grant remarked as he helped her out of the limousine. A mischievous grin played hide-and-seek in his mustache.

"We don't have an order with Arthur Pickens. He's in export-import, isn't he?" She could not take her eyes off the window. Backlit, the batik glowed like stained glass. It made the bikini look twice as stylish as it actually was.

The door of Arthur Pickens International opened, and a tall, graying man stood on the threshold. His face looked as if it had stopped a lot of boxing gloves, but he wore a suit the way old money does. The combination of roughness and class had something in common with Grant's appearance.

Nicole looked from one to the other. "Old friends?"

"None older." The drawl was pure North Carolina. Arthur Pickens took her hand in a well-manicured paw. "Nice to meet you, ma'am. Grant has told me a lot about you."

"Should I be worried?" she asked with a twinkle.

"If I could get somebody to write advertising copy for me that's as complimentary as what this fellow says about you, ma'am, I'd be a billionaire."

Grant, who had been speaking with the driver, joined

them. He gave Nicole a playful pinch on the waist as he slipped an arm around her. "Hello, Pick."

"I detect a trace of a Southern accent," Pickens said to Nicole. "An ex-Southern belle?"

"Tennessee, near the Georgia line. But that was a long time ago."

"A Southern belle, but not a ding-a-ling, I'll bet." Pickens winked. They all laughed as he shepherded them inside. Nicole liked him at once.

Crossing the showroom, she yearned to browse among the racks of intriguing clothes, cases of jewelry and china, and shelves of art objects, as several clients were doing. But Pickens ushered them into a chrome and suede office at the back. Immediately Grant asked about the marlin mounted over the desk. As Pick recounted its capture, Nicole strolled over to a grouping of pictures on an adjacent wall. There was a black-and-white photograph of hunters around a campfire, among which she recognized a much younger Pickens and a thinner, clean-shaven Grant; a framed diploma from Duke University; Pickens and two other men in fatigues standing beside an Army helicopter; a wedding party: Pickens the groom, a laughing brunette for the bride, Grant as the best man, looking bored or maybe a little drunk, and a coolly beautiful redhead as the matron of honor. Instinctively Nicole knew it was Risa, Grant's ex-wife. There were also snapshots of two children and one of a yacht, but Nicole only glanced at those. Pickens and Grant were sitting now, still talking about the fish. Nicole scrutinized Risa again. She and Grant looked as if they belonged together. Yet apparently they had not shared enough to want to keep on sharing.

Nicole took the chair beside Grant and tried to look alert. But inside she was suddenly tired, as if her blood sugar had dropped. Love was so complicated.

She gripped the chair arms. Love was not part of her plan. She had been keeping the word at bay, pushing it below the surface of consciousness. Now that it had escaped, she was afraid she wouldn't be able to imprison it so easily again.

"I'll get right to the point, Nicole, if I can call you by your first name," Pickens said.

"Please. And I can call you—?"

"Pick. That's what my friends call me. Grant came through here a couple of weeks ago and just happened to show me some things he'd bought for his sister Delia." He took a Seawinds blouse out of a desk drawer.

"Just happened to?" Nicole arched an eyebrow at Grant.

Grant folded his arms and tilted his chair back on two legs. "Yep. But now this is between you and Pick."

"I took a look at Seawinds several years ago," Pickens continued, "but the merchandise didn't have the quality it does now." He held up the blouse. "Look: careful execution, good grasp of the basics of design, the crackle effect used with restraint. And the wall hanging tells me that your people have a pretty sophisticated understanding of color and dye combinations. It's become more art than craft."

"You don't know what it means to hear you say this," Nicole said warmly. "We've worked so very hard to bring the quality up and to find new approaches. Sometimes I've wondered if anybody notices."

"Well now, that's partly a marketing problem, as I'm sure Grant has told you. Why hide your light under a bushel? Your batik can compete with anything that comes out of the Orient. As a matter of fact, the simplicity and boldness of the designs probably makes yours more appealing to contemporary tastes. You need to consider wider distribution."

"There's an outlet in Palm Beach. And Percentie's, here on Bay Street, shows our work."

Pickens shook his head. "Palm Beach is all right, but not the place here. You don't want to put Seawinds down

among the souvenir shops and the It's-Better-in-the-Ba-
hamas T-shirts. It's too good for that."

"So what are you suggesting?"

"My wife and I travel all over the world looking for
examples of fine workmanship. We have a string of stores
like this one plus our World Bazaar catalogue." He handed
over a thick, glossy book.

"I've heard of your stores, but I've never seen this,"
Nicole told him, flipping pages.

"We want the best in handicrafts, nothing mass-pro-
duced: *molas* from the San Blas Indians, Chinese jade
carvings, hand-knotted rugs. My question to you is, why
not make Silver Cay batik as well known as Aran Islands
fishermen's sweaters? I can do that for you."

"I suppose you think I should have gone after a bigger
market before now."

"Not at all. You concentrated first on quality instead
of volume, and that's the right way to go about it. But
now it's time for you to stretch yourself a little."

"Your friend is quite persuasive," Nicole said to Grant.

"Pick can sell ice to the Eskimos. Or thinks he can,"
Grant drawled. He was obviously enjoying himself.

"Will you think about hooking up with us?" Pick
pressed.

"I'll have to discuss it with Mr. Gresham, the owner,
and eventually I'll need more information. But on the
face of it, this looks like a wonderful opportunity for us.
Of course you understand that batik is a painstaking process and I can't sacrifice quality for speed. I'll need more
people and the time to train them. And somebody else
at the executive level." She felt herself getting excited.

"Some of those contingencies are dealt with in a certain report," Grant pointed out casually.

"You mean you've been leading Seawinds toward Arthur Pickens International from the beginning?" Nicole
demanded.

"Just looking ahead."

"Which is to say, manipulating me, managing me—"

"With kid gloves, darling."

Pickens guffawed and slapped his knee.

"Oh, all right." Nicole laughed. "I probably would have resisted if you'd thrown the whole master plan at me all at once."

"Out of sheer stubbornness," Grant told Pick in a comically broad Southern accent. "She's as independent as a hog on ice."

"Maybe," Nicole admitted, "but don't forget this. Yes, it will be good for Seawinds to expand. And yes, it will be good for Silver Cay, because it will mean more jobs. But when you're long gone, Grant Sutton, I'll be stuck with all the extra work and responsibility."

A meaningful look passed between Grant and his friend. They both rose to their feet.

"Grant tells me you two only have a limited time here, so I don't want to take up any more of it," Pick said. "Take the catalogue with you and get in touch with me if you want to pursue this." At the door, he clapped Grant on the shoulder. "Grant, old boy, always a pleasure. And may I compliment you as usual on—"

"—his taste in women?" Nicole guessed and knew at once she'd hit it. "I do hope I live up to the grand tradition."

"No, no, I meant . . ." Pick floundered.

"I'll be in touch, Pick," Grant said absently, as if he hadn't heard the exchange.

But when they were back in the taxi, which had waited for them, he began gravely, "About what Pick said—"

Nicole put a finger to his lips. "It doesn't matter. Yesterday you told me to forget my past and to live in the present. Okay, let's forget your past, too. And let's forget the future, above all. We have two days. Forty-eight hours. And the sand in the hourglass is running right now."

"You know something? You are one special lady." He sounded so sincere that she couldn't help feeling a little guilty.

The taxi wound down to Bay Street, the principal thoroughfare, and turned west. Fresh-fruit stands and straw displays that had spilled over from the straw market in Rawson Square narrowed the sidewalks. Risqué T-shirts and embroidered *guayabera* shirts flapped from shop doorways; store windows glittered with gifts from the sea: pearls, black and red coral, pink conch shell jewelry. It was gaudy, it was Bahamian, it was stimulating. Directly in front of them rode a black Mercedes bearing the license plates of the prime minister. As they swept around the British Sheraton Colonial Hotel and the ocean came in sight again, Nicole felt a rush of joy at how fascinating life was.

"Cable Beach?" she asked.

"Farther out."

They passed old Fort Charlotte. The city thinned out and was gone. Everything she saw was a surprise, yet nothing was. Everything was somehow in tune: the sun and water, the scenery, the motion, herself and Grant. A feeling of great tenderness captured her and she rested her cheek against his shoulder. He put an arm around her with an answering tenderness but stayed with his thoughts.

They curved around Goodman Bay and came up fast on the luxury hotels of Cable Beach. There were more flowers here and a satisfied air of expensive, deserved vacations. After that, trees closed in around the road. Down winding drives, behind fences and a screen of trees and vines, Nicole glimpsed sparkling villas and condominiums. At a greenish iron gateway they turned in. For a space of fifty yards, jungle engulfed them. Then they burst out into the open and Nicole saw a white Colonial-style building of several floors. As they wheeled around the drive, she spotted a discreet sign among the bougainvillaea: CARIB SUN.

A boy with a gold front tooth, whisked their baggage away.

Inside, Grant collected mail at the desk and nodded to a couple crossing the lobby. In the elevator, he punched the button for the top floor.

"I own an apartment here," he told her.

"I was wondering where you kept your clothes."

"It's not home. It's an investment."

"Like the hunting cabin in North Carolina?"

"That's right."

The elevator stopped and the door slid back.

"Whoever put you together left out the nesting instinct," Nicole joked as they walked down the hall.

He didn't take it as a joke. "Men don't have a nesting instinct. It's learned behavior. Reluctantly learned." The boy who had taken the luggage was coming out of Number 703.

"Too bad you didn't know Barry. I'm beginning to think you two would have gotten along."

"Is that an insult or a compliment?" He threw open the door.

"Just a fact."

He gave her a straight look. "I'll file it." With a flourishing gesture toward the door, he became charming again. "Welcome."

As soon as she stepped into the living room, her attention flew to the oceanside wall, which was entirely glass. Sea and sky poured into the room. She went to stand in front of the window.

"I see the ocean every day, but there's always a new way to look at it. This is marvelous."

"So are you."

He had come up behind her. She turned and was in his arms.

"Hold me. Just hold me."

He held her. Things unspoken flitted around them, like moths in the night.

Finally Grant kissed her on the nose and asked, "How about a swim and lunch down there?"

Below, several Carib Sun residents lounged around an Olympic-size pool.

"I'd like that."

"Go ahead and change. Your suitcase will be in the bedroom. I need to make some calls."

She left him talking to a corporation in Atlanta. In a few minutes she returned wearing her bathing suit. Over it, like a Malaysian pareu, she wore a wide square of Seawinds batik wrapped tightly about her torso. She carried a towel over her shoulder. Grant was speaking to someone in Spanish, and was taking notes.

Nicole wandered around looking at things. The apartment was beautifully and tastefully furnished, with much natural wood grain and earth tones. Modular furniture upholstered in a nubby cream fabric was scattered about like blocks of limestone. But Grant had made little attempt to claim the place as his own. It was merely a warehouse for the collection of scuba gear by the door, the stacks of old business journals, the water skis leaning in a corner, the tennis racquets on the dresser. She grinned. The clutter was endearing. In the kitchen a framed detailed map of the ocean floor hung over the table. Automatically she picked out the Tongue of the Ocean, off Andros. She strolled back into the living room, absent-mindedly smoothing the pareu over her hips.

Still talking, Grant, leered at her and kissed his fingertips, like a comic opera Italian appreciating a woman, or a plate of spaghetti.

Nicole pranced over to stand in front of him. He made

a grab for the pareu. She scooted back, just out of reach, and batted her eyelashes at him.

He crooked a finger at her. *Come here,* he mouthed. Rapid-fire Spanish poured out of the phone.

Nicole advanced a couple of inches and halted. With an impish bump and grind, she pulled the towel off her shoulder and tossed it to him.

He caught it, chuckling, then had to scramble to catch up with his note-taking.

Nicole paraded in a circle, hands on hips, swaying seductively, and came back to a point just out of his reach. Showing one leg through the slit in the pareu, she winked at him.

He lunged at her, dropping his pen, but she danced out of reach.

She could tell that he was having to ask the other party to repeat. Giggling, she inched closer. With a Brigitte Bardot pout, she started unwrapping her coverup.

Grant fell back in his chair, clutching his chest, feigning some kind of attack, but he kept up his end of the conversation.

Nicole got the pareu off without exposing any more of herself. Holding it up like a curtain, she peeped over it, blowing kisses.

He was back taking notes, rapping out questions, and nodding briskly at the answers. He looked totally absorbed. Apparently he had lost interest in the game.

Nicole crept closer. No reaction. She took another step.

Grant jerked the cloth out of her hands and held it triumphantly over his head, grinning from ear to ear. When he returned to his conversation, he was stumbling over words.

Nicole did a wide-eyed silent-movie pantomime of a woman in distress. Then, eyeing him slyly, she undid the knot at the nape of her neck, which held up the straps of her suit. She gave him a sultry stare and twirled one strap at him.

With a quick farewell, Grant slammed down the phone and surged out of his chair. Squealing, Nicole turned and ran. She yelped as he snapped the towel and it stung her thigh.

Running into the bedroom, she tried to slam the door on him, but he crashed in and grabbed her. The momentum carried them onto the bed, where they collapsed in a tangled heap, laughing too hard to speak.

"You little devil," he finally gasped. "It's a good thing you aren't my secretary. I'd never get a lick of work done."

"It's a good thing you aren't mine, either."

"Sorry. Your body keeps making me forget that your brains are executive material."

Nicole tried to look innocent. It wasn't easy because of the way he was lying on her. "I just wanted to go swimming."

He ran a hand down her thigh. "This hasn't increased your chances. Not immediately, anyway."

Nicole put her arms around him and sighed elaborately. "Well, if there's really something else you'd rather do . . ." She paused for a kiss, then asked, "And when are we going to see more of Nassau?"

"Hard to say. There are people who go to Niagara Falls on their honeymoon and never see the falls." He started unbuttoning his shirt.

"Then we might as well have stayed at my cottage. I wouldn't have had to endure that plane ride."

"Flying is good for your character." He tossed the shirt aside and took her in his arms again. "Prepare for takeoff."

CHAPTER SEVEN

"ONE WHISKEY AND SODA, one white wine." The waiter put down pasteboard circles that read PRIVATEER RESTAURANT AND LOUNGE, set the drinks on them, and left.

With a relaxed smile, Grant settled back in his chair and stretched his long legs out under the table. Raising his glass to Nicole, he drank.

She sipped her wine and looked out over the oily nighttime sheen of the harbor. The Privateer was a low-ceilinged open-air restaurant with its own boat landing tucked into the Nassau waterfront. Hanging ship lanterns cast wavering magic over the dining room, which at eight o'clock was full. In the lounge in the next room a foggy tenor sang "You'll Never Know" to a tinkly piano accompaniment.

Nicole caressed the skirt of her new dress, a floaty sea-green chemise that felt like rose petals on her skin. They had bought it that afternoon in an arcade near Prince George Wharf, after their very late lunch and swim. Her mind trailed lazily back over the day. She was content.

"What are you thinking?" Grant asked.

She realized she had been staring at the water for a long time. "I haven't thanked you for introducing me to Pick. You didn't have to. Rustling up clients for us wasn't part of your job description."

"There's a word for it. *Lagniappe*: 'a small gift given to a customer with a purchase.'"

"The customer is highly satisfied."

"But that isn't what you were thinking."

"Not exactly," Nicole confessed. "I was trying you out in a new context. Of course I already knew about your growing up in North Carolina, but I really didn't connect you to the good ol' boy network until I met Pick. Not much Southern charm comes through when you're talking business. How I hated you that first week!"

He chuckled as if nothing could have pleased him more. "And now?"

She dimpled. "I don't hate you. Not quite."

"I'll have to say that I've revised my first impression of you, as well." He rolled a swallow of whiskey on his tongue. "It's been sort of like watching Lois Lane step out of the Superman comic and become a real person."

"Does that make you Clark Kent, and thus Superman?"

"Nope. I'm not modest enough or sufficiently pure in heart."

"I agree. Besides, I have a better way to characterize the situation," said Nicole. "I think my transformation has something to do with being abducted by a privateer."

"A privateer? Not a pirate?"

"In another century you would have been a privateer," Nicole insisted playfully. "Is that why you chose this restaurant? Anyway, as I understand it, a privateer has the soul of a pirate and he does the things a pirate does, but he's been commissioned to plunder and destroy by his government, during a state of war."

"You mean I'm dangerous, but legally so?"

"Something like that." She laughed.

"Not a bad assessment."

The waiter floated up to take their orders. Grant gave the particulars of two prime rib dinners, then returned to the subject in a more serious vein. "I'm not in a gentleman's game, Nicole. I'm paid to find the weak spots in a company. Many times the problem is simple inefficiency. But all too often, corporate flaws mirror the character flaws of the people who run the corporation. Charm, when I use it, is a trap, a trick to get the information I need. Over the years, I've learned more about the dark side of human nature than I care to know."

"But why do people hire you if they have something to hide?"

"Lots of reasons, mostly having to do with wanting to make more money. And my employer doesn't always anticipate the results. For instance, a man hires me to show him how to squeeze more revenue out of his operation. He doesn't realize that I'm going to discover that his partner of twenty years and the godfather of his children has been embezzling company funds for a decade." He waved a hand. "That's a homey example. I could give you more sinister ones. I've even been asked to help engineer a cover-up of violations of federal regulations."

"I don't care to hear more examples. They've made you cynical."

"And disliked in some quarters. But respected, always respected." For a moment his face was a mask of cold satisfaction. Then he smiled fleetingly. "Of course, once in a while I run across a clean, honest outfit like Seawinds, where the only flaw is the timidity of its manager. A timidity, I confess, that I find refreshing, even though it's bad for business."

Nicole watched the silver wake of a passing launch crawl toward the restaurant. She was thoughtful until it slapped against the pilings under them. "Don't you wish sometimes that you could go back to a more innocent time in your life, when you didn't know so much?"

"Innocence doesn't pay the rent, and being sentimental about it is a waste of time."

"You're a hard man, Grant Sutton."

"A hard man is good to find," he cracked.

The waiter brought hot rolls and butter.

"Sometimes I wish I could escape from Seawinds," Nicole mused. "I love the work, but I get tired. And the responsibility is a heavy burden to bear alone."

"That's what these two days are all about. The great escape, for both of us."

Nicole toyed with her glass. "So after this you go to Caracas. Then what?"

"Then I go other places."

"You're booked solid?"

"For months." The waiter was fussing around again, pouring ice water and setting down hearts of palm salads. Unexpectedly Grant added, "But I'd like to see you again sometime."

"That isn't part of our agreement," she said carefully. "Remember our conversation at the cottage this morning?"

"That was a long time ago. At least a century in emotional time." He grinned winningly. "Besides, I wasn't arguing against having more of the same kind of enjoyment, only against permanence. Agreements can be adjusted, changed, if both parties are willing."

Okay, she thought to herself, if she was going to play her game to win, this was the time to raise the stakes. "People change too, as you said earlier. Maybe Lois Lane has other plans."

"What plans?"

Her mouth had gone dry. She sipped wine. "After you left Seawinds, I started dating again."

"Congratulations."

"I feel as if I've just awakened from a long sleep, like Rip Van Winkle or Sleeping Beauty. I have so much catching up to do, so much to experience." She lifted her glass again. "Thank you for waking me."

"It's been a pleasure. And now that you're awake—"

"I wish I hadn't held myself so aloof from Robert all those years," Nicole went on, as if to herself. "He's been so good to me, and he and Cecile really don't have a marriage. It's merely a merger of two fortunes."

"You stay away from Gresham."

Her eyes widened in genuine surprise. "Why?"

"You don't love him, so don't get involved. Simple."

"I'm involved with you and I'm not in love with you," Nicole pointed out.

"I can change that." His jaw was set like concrete. His eyes were frighteningly dark and deep.

"But haven't you been listening?" she asked with faint insouciance. "I don't want to fall in love. That would be like going back into my prison. I want to be free. Besides, I already told you that you're a terrible risk. Here today and gone tomorrow. Really, I wouldn't fall in love with you if you were the last man on earth."

"Is that so?" He raised an ironic eyebrow. "I suppose it's precisely the qualities that make me such a terrible emotional risk that make me a hell of a good choice to fool around with."

"Yes . . . that's it exactly." In her lap her hands alternately crumpled and smoothed her napkin.

"How wise you are, Nicole. You have all the answers, don't you?"

"I've learned from my mistakes." She faltered, aware that she was losing both her bearings in the conversation and her nerve. "It's too bad that Barry and I didn't work out an understanding like you and I have. It would have saved us both a lot of aggravation."

"Oh? How's that?"

"Well, when I married, I was embarrassingly naive.

I thought that my husband wanted the same things I did: a home, a family, a shared existence. Why else would a man get married? Barry, on the other hand, assumed that I approved of the lifestyle he had already established. Why else, he must have asked himself, would I agree to marry him? All our troubles stemmed from that basic misunderstanding. Now I finally see that we should have had an affair, not a marriage. That would have been very pleasant, as pleasant as this."

"You're too kind."

Ignoring his sarcasm, she plunged on. "You remind me more of him all the time. Oh, you're much more successful than he was and you have drive and flair that he didn't have, but you've got the same elusiveness in personal relationships."

"You mean unreliability, don't you?"

"If you like."

"So if I told you that I love you, if I asked you to marry me, if I said that you were just what I've been looking for and that I wanted to spend the rest of my life with you, you wouldn't believe me?"

In agony, she hesitated. But of course he must be setting a trap for her. He was smiling.

"No. You're joking." Her heart froze. "Aren't you?"

"If you say so." He kept smiling inscrutably. "If you say so." He flagged down the waiter and said something about wine. "Now," he resumed briskly, "you'll have to straighten out a contradiction for me. You say you want freedom. Then whatever became of your dream of the house in the suburbs plus station wagon plus kids plus dog? The dream Barry wouldn't share with you?"

"Forget it. I have, except for a weak moment once in a long while. I don't expect to find it. I'm not even looking."

"Why not, if that's what you want?" he persevered.

"Because I'm hard to please," she snapped. "Because

the kind of happiness I want doesn't exist in real life."
She passed a hand over her eyes. "I'm sorry. Can we
talk about something else?"

"Of course. I aim to please. That's what I'm here
for." His eyes were flat and empty now.

The prime rib roast arrived on a cart, to be carved at
their table. Grant watched the waiter with polite interest
while Nicole stared at the table top and tried to pull
herself together. Everything she had told Grant was the
truth. So why did she feel like a liar? And why did she
feel that he had indeed trapped her? Had she won this
hand or had she lost it? A bell rang somewhere on the
water. The tenor was improvising variations on Duke
Ellington's "Solitude." A man at the next table was trying
to decide whether or not to buy a new cabin cruiser. The
waiter went away. Grant took her hand and held it silently. Then he turned it over and kissed the palm with
a tenderness that had no place in the present conversation.
He had resumed complete control of the evening. Maybe
he had never lost it. She was out of her league.

As if on cue, he said, "We're getting too serious.
Let's see. Did I ever tell you about the time the brakes
went out on my MG when I was going down Lookout
Mountain, at night, in a rainstorm?"

She pasted on a smile. "No, you didn't. Tell me.
Humor me."

Throughout the excellent dinner, Grant kept up a funny
monologue. It was impossible not to laugh and feel better. He could charm the birds out of the trees. After a
second glass of wine she felt thoroughly relaxed, though
she said little. From her point of view there was nothing
more to say. She was neither happy nor sad, but wistful.
For better or worse, they had passed a point of no return
in their nonrelationship. Nothing could develop now. The
last two lines of her favorite Millay sonnet kept coming
back to her:

    I only know that summer sang in me
    A little while, that in me sings no more.

    If Grant noticed her dampened spirits, he gave no sign. When they had finished dessert, he asked, "Do you like Blue Mountain coffee?"

    "From Jamaica? I've never been lucky enough to run across any. I know that it's supposed to be the finest coffee in the world."

    "It's among the scarcest, as well. There aren't more than eight hundred to a thousand bags produced a year. Most of it goes to Japan, with the remaining fraction to the U.S. However, I happen to know that the Privateer has it, though it's not on the menu." He summoned the waiter for a brief exchange. "He'll bring it to us in the lounge. Let's move in there."

    She was so grateful to bring the meal to a close that she could have wept.

    For some time they had been aware of applause, laughter, and an entertainer's patter punctuating the music. Now, as they entered the crowded room, Nicole saw that the pianist was spotlighting people in the audience and using them in his routine.

    They took a just vacated table on the edge of the dance floor. Under a ceiling of low-hanging fishnet, several couples danced to "We've Only Just Begun." Light from kerosene lanterns, flickering through the smoky blue haze, invested random details with secret promise: a bare shoulder powdered with silver; the cut of white linen trousers worn by a man with an eye patch; long, painted nails cradling a champagne glass; a furtive kiss. Grant moved his chair and their knees touched. Another line from the same poem whispered to Nicole:

    And in my heart there stirs a quiet pain

A hand slipped two cups of coffee in front of them. She lifted her cup, closed her eyes, inhaled, drank. "What do you think?" he asked.

"It's delicious. Like sun on a garden. Very mellow."

"You look mellow. Your color is high. Your eyes are magnificent tonight." He was confident and merry.

"Thank you. It's probably the wine." But it wasn't. She knew that he was only seeing what it pleased him to see. A privateer's lady was required to be beautiful, entertaining, and amiable at all times. Otherwise she'd be tossed overboard. Disappointment filled her like a sad perfume. She had believed Grant's coldness to be a front. She was finding out that he was solid ice.

The song ended. Mopping his forehead and jowls with a red silk handkerchief, the pianist chuckled into the microphone, "I'm batting a thousand. I can tell 'em every time." He thrust his head forward and made a great show of scrutinizing the faces of the crowd. "Let . . . me . . . see." The drummer started a roll. The pianist nodded knowingly. A woman laughed, high and nervous. The drum roll built. Talk died.

"Aha!" The pianist's arm shot out, index finger pointing. "Couple at table fourteen, the lady in white. Will you come to the microphone, please?"

"Oh, look." Nicole touched Grant's arm. "They're so young."

"What?" Grant was frowning to himself and taking a pen out of his shirt pocket.

A mere boy and girl, or so they appeared to Nicole, stared into the glare of the spotlight like two possums frozen in the headlights of an oncoming car. When the girl put a hand to her cheek in shock, all the light in the world seemed to catch on her ring finger. A sentimental murmur swept the onlookers.

"Come on now, don't be shy!" boomed the pianist.

The boy, grinning and awkward, got to his feet and

pulled the girl up beside him. Blushing, she tried to resist, then settled for twisting a lock of her hair.

Nicole's heart melted. "They look so new, like a pair of brand-new dolls wrapped in cellophane, or the little couple on top of the wedding cake." She turned to Grant with a surge of emotion and instantly realized that she should have known better. He was chewing on an end of his mustache and jotting figures on a napkin. As she watched, he took out a pocket calculator and hunched forward, figuring in earnest.

"Grant—"

"Not now."

The young couple straggled to the piano, the boy beginning to enjoy himself but the girl still knock-kneed with embarrassment.

"Where you from, man?" the pianist demanded.

The boy allowed that they were from Buffalo, New York.

"And how many children do you have?"

The girl giggled into a tiny hand.

"None so far." The boy's ears reddened.

"We have ourselves a pair of newlyweds, right?" the pianist shouted.

They bobbed their heads. Applause. Cheers. A riff on the drums.

"Batting one thousand, batting one thousand and one," the pianist crooned. "Another round of applause for Mr. and Mrs.—?"

"Zimmer."

The spotlight on the two turned an intense blue. The pianist built a cadenza as solid as a crystal staircase and moved from the top of it into the theme from Zeffirelli's *Romeo and Juliet*. The Zimmers edged onto the empty dance floor.

As soon as they began to move, their bashfulness left them. When they were in each other's arms, the rest of the world disappeared. Nicole's eyes misted, not for the young couple, but for herself. She remembered being like that. Only first love could be that blind. Something jogged her elbow and she glanced at Grant. Business was blind, too, and deaf. She knew Grant didn't even hear the music. He was whistling tunelessly and adding rapidly on the calculator.

"Your interest in the happy couple is touching," she needled him, as some of her spirit returned.

Grant shoved back his chair.

"Are we going over to wish them well?" she persisted.

"That would be a triumph of hope over experience," he said dryly. "No, I have to make a phone call."

"Business at this hour?"

"It can't wait. Excuse me."

Other dancers joined the bride and groom. Nicole passed the time drearily, trying to spot other honeymooners. Since Nassau was a favorite playground for newlyweds from the States, she selected several candidates. She and Barry had spent their wedding night on a jet, traveling from the civil ceremony in California to Florida, where Barry was to start his new job the next day. They had always meant to have a honeymoon later, but somehow the dream had lost importance as time went by. When things had been especially strained between them, Nicole had believed that if they could just go away together and give each other uninterrupted attention, they would find the spark again. She propped her elbows on the table and rested her chin on her palms. How simple she had been in those days. Now she and Grant were giving each other plenty of attention and they certainly had found a spark. It didn't add up to much.

Two songs later, Grant bent over her, his eyes shining with controlled excitement. "Sorry. That took longer than I thought. May I have this dance?"

"You look as if you've had good news."

"Neither good nor bad at this point. But interesting. Very interesting."

They danced the way they always did, in complete accord. Nicole floated in the circle of his arms, loving his sureness and control. But in the back of her mind, she heard the whisper of sand running through an hourglass. They had only one more day together. She had made sure of that.

"The tall gentleman with the lovely blonde! Yes sir, you sir. Come on over here and tell us about yourselves!"

The spotlight swung on them.

"Oh no." Nicole clutched Grant's arm. "Hey, wait a minute. What are you doing?"

He was pulling her toward the dais. He looked down at her with pleasant malice. "Come along, my sentimental friend."

"No! Just tell him we're not—" She broke off, suddenly realizing that she wasn't wearing a ring. For one panicked instant she couldn't remember why she wasn't. But of course, Grant had wrenched it from her hand when they were making love at her cottage. She hadn't given it a second thought until now, after all those years of wearing it waking and sleeping. It must still be lying in her bedroom, wherever he had tossed it. She clasped her hands together to hide the nakedness.

"Good evening, good evening," the pianist greeted them. "I've got a perfect record tonight. Don't let me down. I can pick the bride and groom every time. You've all got that certain something. Don't they have it?" he demanded of his audience. The audience chorused that they did. The pianist sized Grant and Nicole up with eyes like a pair of tired raisins. He smiled oily encouragement. "How long you been married?"

"Fifteen years," Grant replied promptly. He put his arm around Nicole and thrust out his chest.

Catcalls and groans from the onlookers.

The pianist threw up his hands, flashing his rings. "Can't win 'em all!"

"But we are honeymooners," Grant said earnestly.

"I've brought Myrtle here on a second honeymoon, to have some time away from the children and our invalid dog. All the way from, uh, Serendipity, North Carolina."

Nicole dug him in the ribs. It only made him look more sincere.

"Now that's more like it," the pianist crowed. "How many children we talking about?"

"Seven," Grant reported. "Naturally, we drive a station wagon. And there's another one on the—" Applause drowned him out.

Nicole stepped on his toes, hard. "Get me out of this."

"I can't help myself," he whispered. "I crave the lime-light. Ever since you got me up on that runway." The pianist started playing "The Second Time Around."

Under cover of music Nicole spat out, "You scoundrel. Making fun of me, of my values. Of lots of decent people!"

"Madame, you cut me to the quick." He twirled an end of his mustache like an old-time villain.

Nicole stepped up to the piano. "I want him to sing to me," she told the pianist in a loud voice. "I want Gr...uh, Homer, here, to sing me a song." She smiled at Grant. The look of surprise and irritation on his face was worth a thousand honeymoons.

The audience was eating it up. A laughing woman dropped a glass and there were shrieks all around when it shattered. The pianist nodded rhythmically, chuckling to himself. He winked at Nicole to let her know he wasn't fooled. As long as it was good entertainment, he didn't care who they pretended to be.

"What you gonna sing, man?" he asked Grant.

Grant cleared his throat. "Well, uh, I haven't done much singing in recent years, what with the long hours I put in on our turtle farm..." He started to scowl but changed his mind. Stepping in front of Nicole without looking at her, he held a whispered consultation with the pianist.

Nicole folded her arms and waited, tapping a foot nervously. She expected a joke: "Old MacDonald Had a Farm," maybe, or "Row, Row, Row Your Boat." Were there any songs about turtles?

The pianist started a soft, perfectly respectable introduction.

Grant unhooked the microphone from its stand. He turned to Nicole, his face solemn. The spotlight expanded and took on a pearly glow. A hush fell. He began to sing the old Nat King Cole classic, "Unforgettable." A chill ran down Nicole's spine. He was going to play the scene straight.

He sang in an untrained but resonant baritone, a singing-around-the-campfire kind of voice that made you want to sing along. He sang that she was unforgettable though near or far, and that like a song of love that clung to him, how the thought of her did things to him...

His eyes were not joking. When he held his hand out to her, he wasn't doing it for laughs. She clasped his hand. It was hot, dry, and trembling imperceptibly.

She was unforgettable in every way, he sang, his eyes promising her that he meant it, and forever more, that's how she'd stay...He pulled her closer and slipped an arm around her waist. Nicole held on to him and looked out over the lounge. People were drifting in from the restaurant, drawn by the new voice. The pianist went into the interlude. Grant swayed to the music, moving her with him, just as entertainers did while waiting to sing again.

"Doesn't anything faze you?" she asked without moving her lips.

"Yeah." He watched the crowd. "You."

"What do you mean?"

He didn't answer, but started singing again on exactly the right note, in a reprise of the entire song. But this time he sang softer, more intimately, looking down at her. And in spite of her certainty that it was all an act, in spite of the fact that he had to be paying her back for some of the things she had said at dinner, she could feel them slipping away together, past the smoke and the faces, to a place all their own...

Tumultuous applause broke the spell.

"Myrtle, you take him home in a hurry or I be out of a job!" brayed the pianist.

Straight-faced, Grant replaced the microphone and bowed to his audience. When he returned to her, another song was already in the air and the dance floor was filling up. Without a word, he whisked her out among the dancers. A flush high on his cheekbones was the only sign that anything unusual had happened.

"You were wonderful," Nicole said.

"I was inspired." His tone was hard to define.

She waited, wanting him to say something to make her go on feeling as she had while he sang to her, as if she meant something to him. But Grant had nothing more to say. "You must have sung in public before," she ventured again.

"Only public showers." He was a million miles away, maybe adding up numbers again.

They danced on.

In desperation she said, "You really know how to shape a song. That is, you sang the words as if you meant them. It was...very effective."

"Of course I meant them. You are unforgettable. Me, I'm unreliable." He spun her out and caught her again.

Stung, she gave up and rested her cheek against his shoulder. This was where her silly game had gotten her so far. Should she go on with it? If she made Grant care for her then broke off with him as planned, then she would win technically but she would lose Grant. Yet if she dropped the game, he would go away anyway and she would still lose. What about the truth? Why not tell him the truth? No, he would never believe her now. The truth was that she had broken the most important rule in her game of revenge. Even an hour ago, she hadn't known it herself: She had fallen in love with him.

CHAPTER EIGHT

"STOP HERE A MINUTE," Grant ordered the driver.

Nicole looked out the window of the taxi. They were at the top of the arching bridge that connected Paradise Island to Nassau proper. Nighttime Nassau stretched out on either side of them, a dragon's hoard of jewels in the cave of the night. Below them wound the sinuous ribbon of the harbor. She thought she recognized the roof of the Privateer restaurant, where they had been the night before.

"There it is." Grant pointed ahead at Paradise Island. "The playground of the wealthy and their admirers. Ever been there?"

"No, but the Van Zandts—you remember, the lawyers—go occasionally." Lights winked among the trees. Luxury hotels and restaurants, white beaches, splashy Vegas-type shows, and the gambling casino waited there.

Grant told the driver to proceed. To Nicole he said,

"I feel lucky tonight. You're going to bring me luck. Do you gamble?"

"Gin rummy for matchsticks is as far as I go. I don't know when to hold and when to fold. Robert's the one who likes the high stakes."

"I know. That's where I first met him, in a poker game."

"Who won?"

"The dealer." He grinned wryly. "There's a fine line between caring too much about whether or not you win and not caring enough. Robert was guilty of the first and I of the second."

At the base of the bridge, the driver stopped at a checkpoint to pay a tariff. As they continued, Nicole tried not to think about her upcoming meeting with Robert. He had foreseen what would happen, had feared that she would succumb to Grant's charms and get hurt. Robert would be disappointed with her, maybe even disgusted. She lifted her chin stubbornly, as if Robert were sitting next to her, giving her the gently reproving frown she knew so well. He treated her like a child. If nothing else, these two and a half days with Grant had reminded her that she was a woman. She would always be grateful for that. And as for getting hurt, maybe it wouldn't happen after all. Since their disturbing evening at the Privateer, she had forced herself to be more realistic. It was emotional suicide to love a man who was incapable of loving back. She was smarter than that. Wasn't she?

The taxi pulled up in front of the casino, and a valet leaped forward to hold the door. Other taxis arrived and departed all around them. Grant took her arm and they passed through the glass doors, following a group in formal evening clothes.

"Oh, look at that," she murmured. The red-carpeted room before them was as large as a football field. Every inch of it glittered with lights, roulette wheels, slot machines, emerald-topped gaming tables, sleek young croupiers in black tie, milling crowds of beautiful people, recreational gamblers, serious gamblers, and ordinary people like herself who had come to be dazzled. "It's almost too much. After all these years on quiet little Silver Cay, this is fabulous."

"Feel like you've died and gone to Disneyland?"

"Can we walk around and see it all?"

"We can do anything you like." He was amused.

"I'm glad I'm with you," she told him as they started to stroll. "This is so overwhelming to me, so foreign to my experience. I wouldn't know what to do if I were alone."

"You wouldn't be alone for long. You're the prettiest woman here."

"And you, sir, are the biggest liar." She stood on tiptoe to kiss his cheek. "But I love it."

Arm in arm they made a leisurely circuit, stopping to watch a wealthy-looking grandmother feed two paper cupfuls of quarters into a slot machine, to watch the hypnotic spin of the roulette wheel, to follow the roll and bounce of dice on the green baize. After a time, Grant bought chips and settled down at a blackjack game.

"Watch for a while and then you can play," he said. "The object is to get a total of twenty-one, or as near to it as possible, without going over. Face cards count ten, an ace counts one or eleven, the rest count their number value. The dealer deals out one card apiece face down, then one card up. A player has the option of standing or asking for other cards one at a time. But the dealer has to stand on seventeen or more; or if he has sixteen or less, he has to draw. Okay?"

"If you say so."

For a while she tried to make sense of it. But the players intrigued her more than the play. What were the stories behind these intensely expressionless faces? Who were the December-May couple, the ones who were betting so heavily? Had they known each other before tonight? And what about the hard-faced matron with the bosomful of yellow diamonds? She looked as if she ate unfriendly dealers for breakfast. And, moving on around the table, where was the fresh-faced preppie couple from? They must have learned blackjack at summer camp. Nicole went back to studying the game. It moved with scary speed. The man next to her, thin and pale, seemed to have forgotten the burning cigarette dangling from the corner of his mouth. As Nicole watched, he turned up his first card beside the second one and mumbled something to the dealer.

"Why'd he do that?" she whispered to Grant.

"He has a pair. He wants to play them as separate hands. Are you enjoying yourself?"

"I love it. But I'm not learning much about blackjack."

Eventually the preppie couple left to cash in their chips and were replaced by two sunburned women in brand-new Seawinds sundresses. Nicole smiled at them with a warmth that bewildered them. On the table, stacks of chips moved this way and that. Cards skimmed about faster than the eye could follow. A handsome young man with a diamond stud in one ear settled down to the serious business of getting rid of his money as fast as he could. Nicole sensed a ripple pass behind the circle of stony faces at his reckless play. In contrast, the couple next to him were pleasant, steady players with well-rested all-American faces that belonged in a fifties situation comedy. Only their sharp eyes belied their expertise at cards.

And then there was Grant. She tried to imagine that she had come to the casino alone and was seeing him for the first time in her life. What would she think of him? Would she speak to him? She studied his three-quarter profile: the thick hair curling over his collar, the straight nose that made him look stubborn, the sardonic slant of his mustache, the eyes that were almost always amused but never happy. Perhaps she would touch his sleeve, admiring how the light sport jacket accentuated the breadth of his shoulders. *Hello, stranger, I think I'm in love . . .*

On the next hand, Grant was dealt an ace and a jack: twenty-one. It didn't affect him.

"Watching you, 'poker-faced' is taking on a whole new meaning," Nicole teased.

"Want to play the next hand?"

"No, I can't think that fast and I don't understand the betting. Am I bringing you luck?"

"Yes, ma'am."

A trumpet fanfare floated over the din. A man in a dinner jacket, with the flowing white hair of a statesman, joined the group. Nicole was sure she had seen his face in a news magazine. She turned to watch the passing parade. At intervals, tight-faced young men in dark suits sidled past, their eyes sweeping the crowd. These, Nicole surmised, must be casino employees, on the lookout for anyone causing trouble. She watched the crowds for a long time, turning back to the game occasionally for Grant's explanations. Then he was collecting his chips.

"The cabaret is about to start," he told her. "We'll—" He stopped, listening.

Nicole heard it too: the sound of a child sobbing.

One of the dark-suited men slid past, searching for the source of the snuffling. The sobbing escalated to bellows. A ripple passed through the crowd in front of them as people stepped out of the way or were jostled somewhere around their knees. All at once a red-haired boy of about four burst into the open space around their blackjack table. His face was mottled and tear streaked. He stopped and threw back his head.

"I want my mommy!" he bawled. "Mommeee!"

While Nicole and everybody else were deciding what to do, Grant knelt in front of the child, whose T-shirt proclaimed that his name was Robbie.

"I'll help you find your mommy, Robbie. Is she outside?"

"Wah! Mommy!" The boy wiped his nose on his arm and left a smear of dirt all the way to his chin.

Grant took a handkerchief out of his pocket and unfolded it. The bouncer Nicole had noticed earlier hulked over Grant and the child. "Kids aren't supposed to be in here."

"I'm handling it." Grant held the handkerchief to Robbie's nose. "Blow."

The boy obeyed. After that, his crying diminshed to sniffles. He eyed Grant with round blue eyes. "What's *your* name?"

"My name is Grant." He dabbed at the dirt on the boy's face. "Do the doors on your car open?" He pointed to the little red sports car the boy was clutching.

"Yes." He showed Grant how the tiny doors and trunk could be pried open with a fingernail.

"How about the hood?"

Robbie showed him how the hood worked.

"I'll bet you have a sister you have to share your cars with."

"Cindy. She's stupid." Calm now, the boy seemed unaware of the throng eddying around them.

"Are you hiding from her?"

"Sort of."

Grant got to his feet. "You fooled Cindy, all right. She's probably given up trying to find you." He held out his hand. "Let's see if she has." Robbie took it. Grant motioned for Nicole to follow.

Why the old softie, she marveled, he likes children.

Robbie's short legs and the crowd made for slow going. "Where's Mommy and Daddy?" he asked again. His lip trembled.

Grant swung him up to sit on his shoulders. "I'd say they're outside. You tell me as soon as you see them."

They left the casino under the watchful eye of the bouncer. Grant looked up and down the drive. Far to the left, three people stood huddled around a policeman. One of them, a girl in shorts who was all knees and elbows, pointed in their direction. All three broke into a run.

"Robbie!"

In his excitement, Robbie brought the metal sportscar down smartly on Grant's head.

"Hey!" Grant lifted the boy off his shoulders.

The family arrived panting. Robbie's mother, who had been crying, gathered him in her arms and squeezed him hard.

"We've been looking all over for you. Where have you been?"

"Cindy said there were video games in there." Robbie puffed, pointing to the casino.

"I did not."

"Yes, you did."

"I did not."

"Yes, you did."

"Boy, Robbie, are you dumb."

Everyone laughed and exchanged names.

"We're staying over there"—Robbie's bearded father waved a hand—"and we were taking a walk before turning in. We stopped to talk to someone and Robbie just vanished. Thanks. Thanks a lot."

"Glad to do it. He's nice kid. But maybe he shouldn't be wearing a shirt with his name on it," Grant said seriously. "It's a little too easy for strangers to get his confidence by using his name."

Nicole smiled. Stuffy, fatherly: it was a new angle on Grant.

With more effusions of gratitude, Robbie's family hauled him off to bed.

"How did you know Robbie had a sister?" Nicole asked.

"He was wearing pink socks. They could only have been hand-me-downs. Delia has two older girls and a little boy that his Uncle Grant has to look out for."

"No dolls for him, I'll bet. A real man's boy."

"That's right. And don't expect me to apologize for it."

They went back inside to claim Grant's modest winnings and to enjoy the floor show. The comic was funny and the singing was polished and the show girls in their feathers and sequins were stunning; but amidst all the flash and glitter, Nicole's thoughts kept returning to Grant and the boy. He was a good man, a kind man. Why was he so determined to be also a solitary man?

It was very late when they found themselves in another black Cadillac limousine on the road back to the Carib Sun. There was no moon. No cars passed them. The air, moist and heavy, smelled of seaweed.

"What a day." Nicole yawned.

"Did you enjoy it?"

"Yes, but do you always play as hard as you work?"

"Harder." He touseled her hair. "You kept up pretty well."

"I loved every minute: the reef we explored, except for that barracuda that kept following me—"

"—a predator after my own tastes—"

"And then that nice lunch by the pool. And the motor scooter ride and climbing the Queen's Staircase to the old fort—I got a good snapshot of you there, and also one at the straw market, when that funny old lady tried to sell you a hat." She sighed with contentment. "And we mustn't forget that wild tennis game with the couple from your building. I'm sorry I'm not a better player."

"What you lack in skill you make up for in competitiveness." His teeth flashed in the darkness. "I'd hate to be on the other side of the net from you if you were any good."

"What a backhanded compliment! Just for that, I'm going to practice."

They turned into the Carib Sun drive. The taxi swerved to miss some gray creature trundling across the road.

But there wouldn't be a rematch, Nicole reminded herself.

While Grant paid the driver, she got out of the car and went to wait at the steps. A butterfly with a broken wing sat on the top step, fanning feebly. She knelt down.

"What are you doing out this late? You're not supposed to get dew on your wings." She coaxed it onto her index finger. "And you're going to get stepped on if you stay here." She carried it to a bougainvillaea shrub beside the steps. "Go on." She tilted her finger and it crept on to a branch. Its antennae waved vaguely.

Grant came up beside her.

"It hardly has the strength to hold on," Nicole said, worried.

He loped up the steps and held the door for her. "It won't last long anyway with that broken wing. Come on."

"How lucky for me that I'm an *iron* butterfly," she said lightly. "Or so I've been told."

Upstairs, Grant tossed his jacket on a chair and headed for the kitchen. "Want a glass of milk?"

"No, thanks."

"It'll help you sleep. We've got to be at the airport early tomorrow."

She dropped her purse on a table. "I don't care whether I get any sleep or not. I've got the rest of my life to catch up on it." She went to stand in front of the ocean view. He went into the kitchen.

Moonlight struggling through the clouds cast an unearthly sheen on the ocean. The scene recalled to mind the ghastly moon-blanched engravings in a book of Longfellow's poems that her father had owned. The mere names of the poems had chilled her fancy before she was old enough to understand the poetry itself: "The Wreck of the Hesperus," "A Skeleton in Armor," "My Lost Youth." She kicked off her shoes and sat down on an ottoman, lost in an old emotion. Shreds of poetry limped through her mind like poor, broken butterflies. She felt quite alone.

After a time she realized that the kitchen light was out. Lit by a single lamp in the foyer, the living room swam in shadows. The bedroom doorway was a black rectangle. She started up from her seat. All at once it felt like the bad nights at Seawinds, when the house-keeper was away and she was alone in the rambling structure, with the wind full of ghosts and her thoughts a quagmire of regrets. Solitude was no quiet pleasure then, but a deep, dark well with slippery sides. She almost ran to the bedroom.

The door to the balcony was ajar, and a smell of bourbon-cured pipe tobacco curled in on the breeze. Cello music played on the radio. Recessed lighting, behind the headboard of the king-size bed, lit the room dimly. Framed in the doorway, Grant stood on the balcony with his back to her. He leaned on the railing, supporting himself on his forearms, and looked out over villa-dotted forest to-ward a silver slice of ocean in the distance. The wind played with his hair and shivered his shirt across his back. A beautiful, sad song of longing hummed in Ni-cole's bones with the voice of the cello. It was almost over. Only a few more hours with him. And this was the perfect way to remember him: standing with his back to her, vital, intense even in relaxation, yet distant, with his eyes fixed on the far horizon. She stood there a long time, memorizing him.

Grant knocked out his pipe and set it on a patio table. As he turned to come back inside, he saw her and frowned. "What's the matter? You look strange, frightened. He approached her slowly and put an arm around her shoul-ders. "You look . . . lost. What—"

"I don't know, I don't know." She raised her face to his. "Just make it all go away."

"Your lips are hot. Your skin is hot," he murmured

against her mouth in the cajoling tone he always used to keep the mood light. "Are you feverish?"

"Maybe that's it." She put her arms around him and arched her neck as he kissed her ear. "We were out in the sun so long this morning." He nipped at her neck and she melted. She was all right now. As long as he was touching her, she couldn't think, couldn't imagine tomorrow's parting.

"I'm afraid," he said, "that I'm going to have to check every inch of you for sunburn. That one-ounce suit you wore today couldn't possibly have afforded any protection."

"Yes." She sighed as he ran his hands down her. "I think that's just what I need." Their lips met again in a kiss that erased everything but the enticing play of electricity on her skin wherever he touched her.

She was wearing a sleeveless linen dress that buttoned down the front. Grant kissed the bare curve of each shoulder with lingering interest. "Oh, yes." He nodded as his index finger traced down her neckline. "Definitely a case for Dr. Sutton." He undid the top button of her dress and extended the line just inside the lace edging of her low-cut bra.

With her hands clasped loosely at the small of his back, she stood leaning one hip into him and looking up through her lashes, wise and provocative. But it was no good. With a catch in her throat she released him and turned her back.

His arms went around her from behind. He put his cheek against hers. "Tell me."

"I don't know how." A breeze from the balcony made her shudder. His hands moved down to span her rib cage, his fingers brushing the undersides of her breasts. He kissed the nape of her neck. She found the words. "What am I doing here, in this unfamiliar bedroom, miles from home, half undressed in the arms of a stranger?"

He caressed her downward, to her waist and below.

"Don't you find it exciting?"

She closed her eyes and leaned back against him. "Yes, but frightening, too."

He didn't say anything for a long while. Then he turned her around. His expression was somber. With a series of light, deft touches he pushed her hair back. He took her face in his hands. "There is a stranger here, of whom you're frightened. But it isn't me. It's you."

"Me?"

"That new, real person you've become, just in the time I've known you: she's the stranger. You don't know how she's supposed to act, what she's supposed to feel. She has emotions the old Nicole didn't have."

"I know how I'm supposed to feel about you," she blurted out and, with a flutter of panic, knew she wasn't going to stop there.

He kept stroking her hair. "Do you?"

"I love you."

His hand fell still. His face was more still. "No, you don't."

It was the last thing she had expected him to say. "I do. I do. I didn't want to fall in love with you, but I have." She started to throw her arms around him, but he caught her gently by the wrists and held her away from him.

"I was the right man in the right place at the right time for you, that's all. You're not in love with me. You're in love with life again. You're in love with love."

"Yes, I'm in love with love and life. But you're the one who made me feel that way."

"And there will be others. You said yourself that you're open to all kinds of relationships now," he reminded her without reproach.

"I didn't know what I was saying. I wanted to hurt you."

"And you don't know what you're saying now. That's what I'm trying to tell you. You don't know what you want at this point. Give it time. In a couple of weeks you'll wonder what all the excitement was about."

"Oh my God, Grant, don't do this to me. I was wrong about that silly agreement. I have to see you again. It can't end after tonight."

He kissed her forehead. "It's late and you're exhausted. Why don't you get some rest? We can talk about this tomorrow."

She sat down hard on the corner of the bed. From that angle he looked ten feet tall. "Oh. I'm beginning to get it. You don't want to take any responsibility for my feelings. If I fall in love with you, it has nothing to do with you. It's a quirk of my emotional condition. That way you can walk away with a clear conscience."

"I'm not trying to hurt you. I'm trying to keep you from getting hurt."

"That's the most transparent brushoff I've ever run into."

He had that look in his eye, the one that meant he wanted to turn her across his knee. "You're only proving my point by getting upset like this. You're confused."

She stood up fast. "How dare you presume to tell me how I feel? You don't know the meaning of the word *love*. All you're interested in is momentary pleasures."

"*Now* you complain. After the pleasure."

She threw up her hands. "Okay. I'm the fool. You've been consistent all the way. I was the one who tried to read something more into you."

"And of course *you* know how *I* feel."

"You've told me often enough," she retorted.

"If you can't stand the heat, get out of the bedroom."

"I will. Thank you for suggesting it." She stalked out, head held high, and shut herself in the guest bedroom. A minute later the door of the apartment slammed. When she was sure he wasn't coming back, she moved all her things out of his room. Then she undressed and went to bed. She was too wound up to sleep. Lying on her back, staring at the ceiling, she felt humiliated and beaten. It wasn't that he didn't love her, she fumed. She should have expected that. It was the way he had thrown her feelings for him right back in her face. Never would she make a mistake like that again. She closed her eyes, but they popped open again. She knew she wouldn't be able to sleep a wink. And so what?

For a long time she didn't sleep. Then she was running down a dark city street. Thick mist swirled around her, so that she couldn't see her feet. The buildings on either side of the pavement were sooty gray and menaced her with open doors, like giant stone faces with mouths agape. Far ahead shone a light, haloed with mist. It was the light she was trying to reach. Nameless shapes slid out of alleys to follow her. She ran and ran, a bubble of terror swelling in her chest. The light receded, glimmering faintly, mockingly. She was alone. She had always been alone. The street narrowed and twisted back on itself, and the buildings drew around her like a smothering cloak. She cried out.

"Wake up. Wake up. You've had a bad dream."

She was sitting bolt upright. Grant was sitting beside her, holding her. As the mists of nightmare thinned and scattered, she saw that he was wearing a terrycloth robe. The digital clock next to the bed said three thirty-six.

"I'm sorry," she choked out. "I didn't mean to wake you."

"No, I'm the one who's sorry." He threw back the covers and got in bed with her.

"I—"

"Don't say anything. We've both said too much already tonight. Just let me hold you."

She buried her face in his shoulder and held on, receiving the steady calm of his body. Something like relief enveloped them, a shared feeling, though she didn't understand how she knew that he felt it too. The last thing she remembered was Grant murmuring in her ear, "We'll talk tomorrow. About lots of things..."

When she awoke, the patch of sky visible through the balcony door was a bleached-out blue. Birds called in the trees. Grant was lying on his side, turned toward her, deeply asleep. She sat up carefully. He looked tired. In the remorseless early light, the lines around his mouth and eyes were deeply etched. She checked the clock. Her plane left in an hour, his for Caracas in two. They had planned to ride to the airport together. But she had a better idea.

Holding her breath, she slid across the bed and got her feet on the floor. When she stood up, Grant stirred and frowned. She waited, motionless, until his face smoothed out again. Then she gathered up her things and slipped out. In a few minutes she was dressed and packed. Writing the note was the hard part. She ruined several sheets of his good stationery before she produced an awkward thank you and good-bye that would have to do. She left it on the kitchen counter, next to the blender.

Downstairs, the attendant in the lobby called a taxi for her and she went outside to wait. It was going to be another beautiful day. The butterfly was gone from the bougainvillaea. The taxi came. As she rode away, Nicole looked back and caught a glimpse of the balcony to Grant's bedroom. She blew a kiss of farewell to her impossible dream.

CHAPTER NINE

JUST AFTER THREE o'clock on Thursday afternoon, Amy came into Nicole's office. "Here are the files you wanted. Mr. Gresham just called."

"He's here?"

"Yes, he'll be down in a few minutes. He's talking to Sam about the repairs on the roof."

"I'll go see him," Nicole decided. "I need a break." She stretched her arms over her head.

"You certainly do. You've hardly been out of that chair all day. And I couldn't believe that you worked the rest of yesterday, after you got back from Nassau."

"They say hard work is the best cure for what ails you."

"Still don't want to talk about it?"

"I will sometime, but not now," Nicole answered. "Thanks for offering to listen, though." She gathered up the things she wanted to show Robert.

"The week Grant was working here and you two were

so rude to each other," Amy said, "I could tell there was a lot going on under the surface. Whenever you walked through the office with your nose in the air, he would practically start to glow. He couldn't take his eyes off you."

"I know you're trying to cheer me up, but I'd rather not dwell on those days right now." Nicole stopped at the door. "Were you jealous?"

Amy reddened. "Yes. I didn't have a chance against you and you weren't even trying. That's never happened to me before."

"And now?"

"Oh well, that's over, isn't it? And Nicole, I met the most gorgeous man yesterday. He's staying at the yacht club and he's from San Francisco and he's blond and we're having lunch together tomorrow."

"You're impossible!" Nicole laughed for the first time that day. "But I wish I could be like you."

"I'll see if he has a friend."

"Oh, stop it! See you later."

She found Robert having coffee in the sunroom. Sam was just leaving.

"Here she is." Robert came to meet her. They kissed cheeks. "Coffee?"

"All right. How've you been, Boss?"

"Busy." They sat down and Robert poured a cup for her. Nicole thought he had never looked better: trimmer than when she had last seen him, more tanned, and dressed with his customary care. But there was an edginess to his movements. "I called on Tuesday," he informed her. "Amy said you were visiting a friend in Nassau."

Good old Amy. "I hope you didn't mind my taking a couple of days off."

"No, no, of course not." He stirred sugar into his coffee. "I didn't know you had friends there."

"And I don't know everything about you, either," Nicole gibed. "Look at this." She handed him the World

Bazaar catalogue. "I didn't spend all my time sunbathing. Have you ever heard of Arthur Pickens International?"

Without looking at it, he put the book to one side. "You went by plane?"

"Yes."

"But you hate to fly."

"I'm still not crazy about it, but I've made up my mind not to let my fear cripple me anymore."

"Hmmm."

"Anyway, listen to me. I met Arthur Pickens himself. He's interested in selling our batik. Can you believe it? Of course, we'll have to talk with him more and ask the Van Zandts about the legalities, but what do you think? Isn't this just the opportunity we've been waiting for?"

"How did you meet this Arthur Pickens? Did you contact him?"

Nicole picked up her coffee. If she answered truthfully, then he would soon figure out that she had spent her little vacation with Grant. Instinctively she shied away from telling him about that. He would ask even more questions, and she had a right to privacy. "I'm a resourceful lady."

Robert lit a cigarette and took a drag from the bottom of his lungs. "Before we get into this Arthur Pickens thing, there are some other matters I'd like to discuss first."

"The Sutton report? I have it right here." She whipped it out of the stack of papers in her lap.

Robert stared at her. "Why are you so jumpy? Have there been rumors out here?"

"Rumors about what?"

"No, I guess there hasn't been time." He hitched his chair closer to hers and knocked ashes into an ashtray. "I want you to understand that I've thought carefully about what I'm going to say, especially about how it will affect you. I care very deeply about what happens to you."

Some papers slid off her lap. She didn't pick them up.

"You know," he continued, "That I bought Seawinds to please what's-her-name." It was one of his little jokes to pretend that he had forgotten his first wife's name. This time it fell flat. "It's an anomaly in my holdings. It bears no relation to anything else I own." He put down the cigarette. "For some time I've been thinking of selling it."

"So that's what it was. I sensed that you were keeping something from me."

"I wasn't trying to hide anything. I just didn't want to worry you without cause, before I had an offer."

"But we're doing so well," Nicole protested. "I wrote you about the new connection with Columbus Tours."

"Yes. The overall picture here is excellent. That's exactly why I can command such a good price."

Nicole steepled her fingers under her chin and thought. "Why did you hire Grant Sutton to do that expensive analysis if you didn't intend to let me follow through on his suggestions?"

"Sutton's seal of approval is priceless. Word gets around very quickly about something like that. His report has actually raised the price of Seawinds." He moved the ashtray a couple of inches forward on the table. "I hope you're not too disappointed to hear this."

"To tell you the truth, I'm stunned. But of course you have every right to sell." She retrieved the spilled papers and put them on a table. "Seawinds really doesn't mean anything to you, does it?"

"Well, I never involved myself in the running of it. I probably would have sold it before now, except that you made it easy for me to keep it, by running things so smoothly. And I always enjoyed coming here to relax . . . and to see you."

"Ironic, isn't it?" She shook her head. "I did my job too well. If I had left Seawinds the way I found it, it wouldn't have been worth selling."

Robert shifted uneasily in his chair. "I guess I didn't realize you'd care this much. I thought it was just a job to you. I had to beg you to take it, remember?"

"That was a long time ago, before it became a part of me. We're like a family here. I know the employees' children. I know their grandparents." She and Grant had talked about her feelings for Seawinds and he had understood them. Strange, she mused, that the man without a home had been able to see why Seawinds was home to her. "Who's buying it? Do you suppose they need a good manager?"

"The deal hasn't gone through yet," Robert explained. "A couple of weeks ago I received the proverbial offer I couldn't refuse. But it's just been topped. We'll have to wait and see where the bidding ends."

She looked at the World Bazaar catalogue, forgotten on an end table, and thought of the difference such a connection would have made to the local economy. She felt like crying. "Maybe nothing will change," she said, brightening. "Are we talking about absentee owners, or will they actually take over operations?"

Robert took her firmly by the shoulders. "You can't think of this as Seawinds anymore. Things will never be the same again. If you were to stay on, you wouldn't have the freedom I've given you. You'd be just another employee."

"Do you expect me to resign?"

"Of course. And they'll expect you to. The new owners will undoubtedly want to fill your position themselves, with someone of their own choosing."

"But what will I do? There aren't that many jobs in Crescent Harbour."

Robert had gone back to smoking. Now he stubbed out the cigarette. "Let me decide. I know what's best for you. I've always known, haven't I?"

"Have you?"

"Come back to the States with me."

"What?"

"I'll give you another job. Any job you want."

"I can't just leave. I have friends, I have my cottage—"

"You'll make other friends. I'll see that you do. And I'll buy you ten cottages if you want them."

"Robert, I don't think I understand what you're saying."

"Don't you?" He rose and went to the big windows that looked out over the uncultivated fields of the estate. "I remember the first time I ever saw you. Barry brought you by the office. You were wearing a yellow dress and a straw hat with a wide brim. Remember?"

She made a vague noise of concurrence. She didn't remember at all.

"Ever since that day I've wished you were mine. But there was always something in the way. You were married, I was married." He turned around. "I can give you everything, more than you've ever dreamed of having. Let me do that, Nicole. Come with me."

"You shouldn't be saying these things. You're still a married man." Guiltily she recalled how she had taunted Grant with this very possibility.

"You know what my marriage is."

"It's still a marriage."

"Not for much longer. We've started divorce proceedings."

"I'm sorry."

"Don't be. I'm not. I should have known better. Marriages of convenience nearly always turn out to be inconvenient." He came back to his chair. "Let me help you get reestablished in the States. We'll continue as friends, just as we are now. Then, after I'm free—"

"Please," she stopped him. "You're asking for more than friendship from the beginning. You know you are."

"Would that offend you? The last thing I want to do is hurt or upset you."

"No, it isn't that, although I certainly could never enter into an intimate relationship with a married man, no matter what the circumstances. The concept of marriage is too important to me." She paused and looked up at the ceiling. There was no easy way to say what she had to say. "I like you very much. You're a good friend. But I don't love you."

"You can learn to love me. Even if you don't, we can be happy. We're compatible. Many couples find contentment without love."

"Another marriage of convenience?"

"You know that isn't what I mean," he replied petulantly.

"Please don't press me in this," Nicole said as kindly as she could. "I can't go with you if I don't love you. It would end badly, sadly. Then we wouldn't even have our friendship. I'm sorry. You don't start a relationship like that hoping you'll end up in love. You have to start with love."

Robert lit another cigarette. "I must say I'm surprised at your attitude. You've always been so . . . open to suggestions about your personal life."

"Don't you mean easy to sway? Yes, that's exactly what you mean. There was a time, and it wasn't long ago, when I would have agreed to go with you, would have tried to learn to love you. I would have been content with the security you're offering. But I've learned something about myself since then, and about love."

He opened his mouth to argue with her. But instead he frowned and picked up her hand. They both looked at the place where her wedding ring had been. Nicole found herself remembering all the times that Robert had brought up Barry, when she hadn't even been thinking of him. Had Robert been deliberately contributing to her imprisonment in her widowhood to keep her away from other men? A dog in the manger, Grant had called him. She sighed inwardly. In any case, she couldn't entirely blame Robert. She had been a willing conspirator in her imprisonment. She stole a glance at Robert. Why was he changing his tactics now? Did he know about her and Grant? The phrase *dog in the manger* repeated itself again. Robert wanted to shift her from one soft prison to another. He only meant her well. But Grant had shown her how to burst out, how to be free. She couldn't go back.

She looked Robert in the eye. "I'm not wearing the ring anymore. And if you sell Seawinds, I won't work here anymore."

He regarded her with awe. "What's happened to you?"

"It's a long story."

She saw that he wanted to ask more but didn't dare. "What will you do here?"

"I'll be fine. I'll be just fine."

The telephone rang in the living room. Robert went to answer it. "It's for you," he called. Glad of the interruption, she hurried in.

"Nicole"—Amy's breathless voice came over the line—"I'm holding a long distance call for you, from Caracas. It's Grant."

"Tell him I'm in conference. He can leave a message."

"Are you sure? I don't think he's going to like that."

"I'm sure. And Amy, if he calls again, tell him the same thing."

Two hours later, after she had closed up the office and had declined a halfhearted dinner invitation from Robert, she drove out to her cottage. When she had returned from Nassau the day before, she had gone straight to the office and then spent the night in her room at Seawinds. The cottage would be as she and Grant had left it.

When she unlocked the door and slipped inside, a

very faint scent of fading iris lay on the still air. She walked through the rooms with a halting step, as if she had never been there before. In the kitchen she picked the champagne cork out of the hanging plant and threw it away. In the bathroom, two towels hung side by side. In the bedroom, Grant's coffee mug still sat on the dresser. She tossed the towels in the clothes hamper and took the mug to the kitchen, where she washed and dried it, then put it away. She went to the door and looked at the ocean, which knew all there was to know about change. She was going to be fine. Nobody had promised her that it would be easy.

CHAPTER TEN

NICOLE PUT ASIDE the inventory sheets, rubbed her eyes, and scooted down in bed. It was nearly eleven P.M and she had been working inefficiently since eight. It was hard to take any interest in the work, because the fate of Seawinds was still undecided. Robert had left two weeks before. Every day she expected to hear who bought the place, but as yet no word had come. The employees were restless, too, wondering if any jobs would be eliminated or if anyone would be replaced. Even Amy, despite the new boyfriend, was subdued.

She adjusted the pillows at her back and picked up her detective novel. It was a good one, set in southern Michigan. The night was muggy and still. She kicked off the sheet. She was wearing an oversized tie-dyed T-shirt, a Seawinds experiment, and it only came a little way down her thighs, but it was too hot. She thought about taking it off, but that meant moving. She was too tired. She began to read. The hero, an ex-private investigator, was getting the stuffing knocked out of him by a psychopathic deputy sheriff. She wondered where Grant was now. The phone calls from Caracas had stopped after two days. The book started to grab her. The scene she was reading was tricky psychologically and before long she was cheering for the hero as he laboriously got the upper hand. On the periphery of her attention, she heard a car approaching. That would be Mamie and Sam returning from visiting their relatives in town, although usually they stayed later. The hero had outsmarted the deputy and was getting away, even though he was handcuffed and injured.

Nicole put the book down. The car had stopped on the circular drive. A door slammed. Mamie and Sam always went around to the back, where they lived. She got out of bed and went to the window. In the darkness she could just make out a Ford sedan in the shadows of the trees. No one was walking around. She couldn't see inside the car. Eager to resume the novel, she went back to bed. Maybe it was a couple looking for privacy.

Downstairs the front door opened and shut. She had locked that door before coming upstairs. She remembered because she had had trouble with the bolt. No one had a key except Robert, the housekeeper, and herself. Robert would not be coming back, although he and she had parted as friends. Mamie never used the front door at night.

Nicole slipped out of bed, threw on a robe, and tiptoed out to the landing. Footsteps rang in the hall, then fell silent as the walker hit the living room rug. A burglar? It was possible that someone had seen Mamie and Sam in town and had figured that the place was empty. Most people on the island assumed that Nicole lived at her beach cottage all the time.

The footsteps returned to the front hall, then took the corridor down to Robert's suite. If she could get to the living room, she could phone the police. But that was

foolhardy. It would be better to slip out the front door
and hide until the intruder had left. Then she could come
back in and phone. Maybe he had left the keys in his
car and she could drive to town. At all costs, she didn't
want to be trapped upstairs. She started down the steps
in the dark, staying close to the wall so that the boards
would be less likely to squeak. Then she remembered
that one of the balusters supporting the stair rail was
loose. She sneaked across the stairs and felt the posts
as she descended. They were of solid wood, over three
feet long and thicker than her wrist. She found the
loose one, pulled it out, and took it with her. Rounding
the curve of the staircase, she had a clear view of the
front hall, where a dim wall light burned. No one was
about. No footsteps sounded. She would have twenty
feet to cross between the bottom of the stairs and the
front door.

By the time she reached the last step, she was beginning to wonder if she shouldn't have remained quietly
in her room. But no, the lock on her door didn't work.
Even now, the intruder might have found his way to the
upper floor via the back stairs and be approaching her
room. A more terrible thought struck her. Maybe it wasn't
a burglar at all. Maybe the person knew she was alone.
Maybe he had come for her.

She dashed across the hall and tugged at the handle
of the front door. It didn't budge. The bolt was on. She
looked around wildly. Still no one. Shoving the baluster
under her arm, she tried to turn back the bolt. It balked.
She pushed harder. The baluster slid to the floor with a
clatter like the crack of doom.

"Going somewhere?"

She looked over her shoulder in astonishment.

Grant sauntered up the corridor toward her. "I'm from
the phone company, ma'am. I've been sent to find out
why you don't answer your long-distance calls."

She swallowed. "It wasn't the phone." Her knees went

weak and she leaned her forehead against the door. "I thought you were a burglar."

"I know it wasn't the phone." He turned her around. "But we do all kinds of repairs. What you need is to have that chip removed from your shoulder. Damn it, why did you walk out on me?"

"I hate long good-byes."

"Then we'll have a long hello." Nothing had changed. As soon as he took her in his arms, she wondered how she had been able to do without him, even for a day. "I've missed you," he said. "Every minute. I don't ever want to be without you again."

"I've missed you too." She kissed him shyly. He had come back to her, for good. She could hardly believe it. But he had said so. The relief nearly dissolved her bones. "That nightmare I had in Nassau, and the rest of it, the fear that last night—it was all because I thought this would never happen again, being in your arms."

He kissed her back, without any shyness and for a long time. "I have a lot to say to you. First of all, I've been the biggest fool in the world."

"No, I am. I retired the title, undefeated, in Nassau."

He gave her a little shake. "Do you know what I felt like when I woke up and found you gone?"

"I hope you felt as bad as I did when I left." She couldn't stop smiling.

"Worse. Because I had hurt you and I couldn't make it right. Until now. I apologize, and I want to clear up a misunderstanding."

"Apology accepted." She closed her eyes and clung to him while the shock finished sinking in. He had come back to her. Things were going to be different. She could feel it. But . . . hadn't she believed that every time Barry had turned up again? She pushed the thought away. Happiness raged in her like a fever. She wanted it to consume her and burn away all doubts. "How did you get away?

I thought you were booked up."

"I canceled left and right."

"You mean I'm costing you money?"

"And time and energy. That's why we're going to straighten this out. I literally can't afford to be apart from you. What do you say we stop playing games?" He stroked her back until she felt like a sleek, sleepy cat. Then slowly she woke up again and found herself hungry for him, hungry for the glorious, reassuring oblivion his lovemaking brought. She never doubted him when she was in his arms.

She loosened his tie. "Do we have to stop the games? I had a certain game in mind."

"Well...maybe that one. It's been a long two weeks." He opened her robe and whistled at the T-shirt. "Good Lord, do you always dress that way for burglars?"

"Just for the good-looking ones."

"You'd knock 'em dead, all right, but it wouldn't be with that bludgeon."

"How *did* you get in here, anyway?" She shrugged and the robe slid to the floor.

"With a key. From Gresham."

"You saw him?"

"Sure, passing through Miami."

Nicole frowned. "Strange. I'm surprised he was so accommodating."

"Uh, about that game..."

After a while Nicole giggled. "Stop it. What if Mamie and Sam come home?"

"Shall we repair to your boudoir, then?"

Arms around each other, they climbed the stairs. She had one bad moment, wondering how they could be together for good. Was he just placating her? Then the wild happiness roared over her again.

"I'm sorry I scared you," he said. "I figured you might be at your beach house."

"I haven't stayed at the cottage since you left. It was too empty without you. Somehow it became yours too, after only one night."

"Here's to more nights." He stopped in the door to her bedroom and hugged her tightly, his head bent over hers. She sensed pain in him.

"What is it?"

"Risa walked out on me, did I tell you that? I didn't walk out on her. In fact I wasn't even there to witness her exit. I was too busy. I said it would never happen to me again."

"So you always left first."

He rubbed her cheek with the back of his hand. "When I found your note, it hurt. Don't look so surprised. I can be hurt. 'If you prick us, do we not bleed?'" His eyes darted around the room as if he were anxious to escape the subject. "So this is your home away from home."

"Pretty austere, isn't it?"

He noted the painted desk, dresser, chair, and bed; the flowered drapes; the pictures on the wall. Barry's picture was still there, but it no longer reproached her. Grant's attention wandered back to the bed. "You have the essentials."

She found that she was nervous, but pleasantly so because the feeling was born of anticipation. "Would you like some sherry? I keep some here for the rare occasions when I'm too tired to sleep, after I've stayed up with the books."

"Fine." He kicked his shoes off and sat down against the pillows on the bed, legs stretched out, hands clasped behind his head. He watched her take things out of the closet. "Just one question. Why do you have two glasses?"

"In case I break one, smartie." She poured the sherry and carried the glasses to the bed. "You're my very first male visitor."

"Gresham never found his way up here?" He lifted

an arm. Nicole tucked herself into the curve of it and drew up her knees. The bed was narrower than she had thought.

"He was here not long ago and asked me to go back with him. He's divorcing Cecile."

"I figured he might make a move, because of the sale."

She drank, washing the warm, nutty taste around in her mouth before she swallowed. "I wonder if he and I can still be friends after this. He was always good to me, but for more selfish reasons than I ever imagined. It almost makes me shudder. All those times we spent together, all those brotherly hugs and kisses, meant something entirely different to him. I wish he had told me how he felt." She gave Grant a playful dig in the ribs. "I always know where you stand, whether I want to or not." Doubt tickled at her again. She drove it away with a laugh.

They clinked glasses.

"To the future," he suggested.

"I thought you didn't like to talk about the future."

"I do now." He set his glass on the nightstand. "I've got tremendous plans. I could do with more capital, but there's enough to get started. Want to hear them?"

"What, you're not rich?"

"Comfortably well-off, that's all. No inheritance except for a little bit of land, and for a long time I spent money as fast as I made it. I never was one to sit on my assets. But this is a different situation."

If he would only hold her tighter, make love to her, make her believe that they belonged together... "I must be losing my touch," she said, playing with the buttons on his shirt. "You never used to want to discuss business at times like this."

"Ah, yes." He took her glass and set it beside his. "Tell the secretary to hold all my calls." He pulled her into his lap. "That garment is positively indecent. I demand you remove it at once." He fondled her breasts, which showed in exuberant detail through the clinging knit.

"Well, I think you're terribly overdressed for this party," Nicole said, and unbuttoned his shirt.

After a bit he finished undressing and returned to where she knelt on the bed. He shook his head. "Do I have to do everything around here?"

"I'll help." She raised her arms so that he could pull her shirt off. Then he pushed her gently back against the pillows. For a time he sat beside her, a hand on her knee, and they simply absorbed the fact that they were together again and that it was going to be good.

He leaned down and kissed her once, twice, without touching the rest of her. He sat back and looked her up and down before leaning over to give each breast a long, licking kiss. The next time he bent over her, it was to turn out the light. He lay down next to her and they came together, so that they lay facing each other on their sides, touching down the length of their bodies. They stayed that way a long time, touching and nuzzling. It was gentler this time, as if she were newly precious to him: a reacquaintance that was so slow it was almost perverse. She lay back in a simmering, lazy ecstasy, one leg thrown over him, stroking his hard body, and let him enjoy her. When she was trembling with readiness, her body a moist, yearning haven for him, he turned her on her back. As he moved over her, she embraced him totally, moaning with pleasure. She bathed his face in hot, urgent kisses, her pelvis nudging at him.

"Are you in the arms of a stranger now?" he asked hoarsely, as the steady, driving movement began.

"Actually . . . expect an answer?" She anchored her fingers at the back of his head and gave herself up to the tremendous surging power, the volcanic push through feeling after expanding feeling.

"Yes."

And just before the last kiss and the explosion that shattered her into a thousand spinning stars, she cried, "Not a stranger not . . . ever again."

Nicole's hand shot out and batted the alarm clock into silence. Then she woke up. The pillow under her cheek was damp with perspiration. Grant was curled around her, an arm cradling her protectively. His breath stirred the curls on her neck. She stretched luxuriantly against him.

He mumbled something that sounded like "Pennsylvania" and rolled on his back.

On the way to the shower, she did a soft-shoe shuffle and slide out of sheer exhilaration.

When she came out later to get her clothes, moving stealthily, he said with his eyes closed, "I can't see you, but I know you're there. Are you a burglar? Just let me get into my T-shirt."

She patted him on the head. "Go back to sleep."

Downstairs in the kitchen, Mamie was making French toast and frying bacon. She and Nicole traded greetings.

"Don't set a place in the dining room," Nicole told her. "I'll have mine on a tray upstairs. I'll fix it."

"Okay." Mamie flipped two slices of egg-soaked bread in the pan of sizzling butter. Crossing to the refrigerator, she stopped to look at the tray Nicole was loading. "Eating for two?"

Nicole blushed and finished pouring the second glass of pineapple juice. "No, I have a . . . guest."

Mamie took out jam and butter. "A guest." Her eyes twinkled. She and Nicole had known each other a long time. "That's nice. How long will he be staying?"

"He? It could be my sister, Mamie."

"It could be. How long is he staying?"

Nicole added silverware and napkins next to the cups and plates. "I don't know, come to think of it. I'll ask. You'll want to know about meals, won't you?"

Mamie shrugged. "I'd think you'd want to know. Anyway, it's nice to see you looking so happy."

Carrying the tray upstairs, Nicole faced facts. She needed to know more about Grant's visit. She had a right to know. Besides, something didn't fit.

He was sitting up, reading her detective novel. "Good book. And good morning."

"It is, isn't it?" Nicole positioned the tray on his lap and sat down beside him.

"You're spoiling me." He grinned. "And on a workday, too."

"A workday? You mean you're leaving? This morning?"

"Of course I'm not leaving. I'm working here."

"You brought paperwork with you?"

Grant crooked an eyebrow at her. "Wait a minute. Don't you know? I thought Gresham told you. I was sure he had."

"Told me what?"

He folded the napkin he had just picked up and returned it to the tray. "Why do you think he gave me a key? I'm the new owner of Seawinds."

CHAPTER ELEVEN

"YOU!" NICOLE EXCLAIMED.

"Yeah, how do you like that?"

"Well . . . I don't know. I mean, congratulations."

Grant dug into his French toast. "I thought you'd be relieved."

"Relieved?"

In high spirits, he snapped his fingers in front of her eyes. "Wake up. You at least knew about the sale. We mentioned it last night. Then you must have been worried about what was going to happen, whether there would be a shake-up in personnel and so on."

"Yes." She was utterly numb, trying to figure it all out.

"Okay, your fears are over. I do have long-range plans, which I was going to tell you about last night, except that we became otherwise involved. But the day-to-day operation will go on pretty much as it has. After all, I have an expert to handle that for me."

"Who?"

"You."

"I see." Apparently she had drunk some juice. The glass in her hand was only two-thirds full.

"I'll want to call all of the employees together for a talk. There's room enough in the studio. How about ten o'clock this morning? Can you arrange it?"

"I suppose." She put down the glass, almost missing the tray. "I want to know more about this, if you don't mind."

"Sure. First question?" He chewed bacon. "Great breakfast. Why aren't you eating?"

"When you first came to Seawinds with Robert, did you intend to buy it?"

"It wasn't for sale. But the idea was in the back of my mind. I'd heard Gresham say that he didn't know why he was hanging on to it. The word was out, more or less. When he hired me, I figured he wanted to find out the company's real worth."

"So you decided to kill two birds with one stone. You could report on the company to Robert and collect a fee for doing so. At the same time, you could make your own private survey and find out if you should buy."

"You're a smart little thing. Are there any more at home like you?" He held up a forkful of French toast. "Open."

She opened her mouth and took the bite. She didn't taste anything. "When did you make your offer?"

"Funny you should ask. When you and I went to see Pick, he mentioned to me that he'd heard an offer had been made for Seawinds. He knew I was interested."

"When did he tell you?"

"While you were looking at those pictures on the wall. He was quiet about it, because he wasn't sure whose side you were on. He thought you might relay my interest back to Gresham and the price could go up. I had an idea I might not be welcome in the bidding."

"Why didn't *you* tell me?"

"It seems to me we've had this conversation before." A crease of annoyance appeared between his eyebrows. "'Whatever concerns Seawinds concerns me' or something to that effect."

"Well?"

"I wanted to surprise you." He punched at her with an index finger. "That's all. So don't go looking for any ulterior motives."

"I'm surprised, all right."

"Pick knew how much had been offered. I figured up what I could do and made a call."

"From the Privateer?"

"I had to move fast. Look, how long is this inquisition going to take? I need to shower and shave and get stuff from the car." He picked up her hand and kissed the palm. "Or, what the hell, the new boss could get to the office late on the first day."

She moved down a ways on the bed. "This time we're not going to let pleasure come before business."

"As you say, madame." He indicated the food. "Want anything?"

"No, thank you."

He put the tray aside, retaining his coffee cup. "Next question?"

His cockiness irritated her more by the minute, but she kept her voice neutral. "One of the things that impressed me about your dealings with us was the extras, such as making the contact with Columbus Tours and with Arthur Pickens."

"Thank you."

"But it was all for yourself, wasn't it? You knew you would step in in time to reap the benefits."

Grant threw off the sheet and heaved himself out of bed. "I'm going to take a shower. I'm telling you before I do it, so it won't come as a surprise to you."

In the shower he sang "Unforgettable" and "You Made

Me Love You," hamming up the latter with a nasal vaudeville vibrato. Nicole sat on the bed and made a waterlily by folding one of the paper napkins. As soon as she finished and set the lily on the tray, it unfolded itself.

In a few minutes Grant came out of the bathroom with a towel around his hips, rubbing his hair dry with another towel. He walked over and sat down beside her. "I know that, effectively, you've been the boss here for a long time. We've talked about that before and I don't intend to interfere with what you do, although I'm going to take more of an interest than Gresham did. It will be a partnership, in every way."

"Exactly how much time will you spend here? Don't tell me you're giving up your consulting business."

"Not entirely. I've spent too much time building a clientele." He patted her on the shoulder. "Smile. You've just had good news."

Nicole got up and went to sit in a chair across the room. Would she ever break out of the pattern? Underpaid and overworked by some gallivanting man? Barry had expected her to run Starr Charter while he partied with rich clients. Robert had thrust upon her total responsibility for a company in which he had no interest. And now Grant expected her to continue to run it under the same conditions, not to mention his expectations concerning their personal involvement. Grant, who had pointed out the self-destructive pattern to her . . .

"Okay," he ordered. "Out with it."

"What if I resign? Robert said I should."

"He would."

"What if I do?"

"That would be sticky. You're one of the big reasons I bought Seawinds. You're its biggest asset." He gathered up his clothes. With a pang, Nicole recalled the circumstances in which he had removed them the night before.

"If you read the deed carefully," she said, "you'll find that the manager isn't one of the fixtures. How dare you assume that you've bought me as part of the deal?"

"Would you have preferred that some stranger buy Seawinds and toss you out on your ear?" he demanded, bristling. "Damnation, I bought Seawinds for you as well as for me."

"Sure you did."

"I have another surprise for you that will prove it."

"Is it as big as this first surprise?"

"At least."

"I don't think I could take another one like that." She stood up. "You knew from the beginning that you wanted to buy Seawinds. Did you also decide then that you had to keep the manager happy, so that you could go on your way and let her do all the work? Is that why we've been having this affair? Oh, yes, we'll never be apart again. How touching!"

"Believe it or not," Grant drawled, "you're not indispensable around here. As a manager, that is."

"Then I resign." She marched to the door.

"Now that I don't have a conflict of interest, can we go on with our affair?"

"You can go to hell."

She had reached the landing when he stuck his head out the door and inquired imperturbably, "Going to the office?"

"To clean out my desk."

"Don't take anything that doesn't belong to you."

She clattered down the stairs and nearly sprained her wrist getting the bolt back on the front door. The door belonged to Grant now. She hoped he had a devil of a time getting it fixed.

Amy was reading the morning paper when Nicole stormed into the office.

"Tell everyone to meet in the studio at ten. Our new owner, Mr. Grant Sutton, wishes to make a speech."

Amy's jaw dropped. "You don't mean it! Why, this is absolutely terrific."

"Is it?" Nicole banged open the door to her office and strode to the middle of the room. There she halted, uncertain what to do. Amy followed her in.

"What's the matter with you? You've missed him, you know you have. Now you can see him all the time."

"Maybe I'll live in Oregon. My sister likes it there."

"You can't quit."

"Watch me. I'll show him. He seems to think I'm joking."

Amy perched on the corner of Nicole's desk and crossed her ankles. "What about the rest of us? Don't you feel any loyalty to the staff?"

"That's probably what he's counting on to keep me here."

"I doubt it. I'll bet he's counting on your feelings for him," Amy observed.

"That's worse."

Amy got up and closed the door. "I just don't understand you. We have a new owner who's a terrific businessman. If anybody can make us famous, he can. Besides that, it's someone you're crazy about and he's more than just interested in you. What in the world is the problem?"

"It's hard to explain." Nicole sat down at her desk. "In the first place, I guess I've been taught a hard lesson in the basics of capitalism. I've come to think of Seawinds as mine, because of all I've put into it. But it isn't mine and it never will be. All of the really important decisions are made without me. I'm not supposed to worry my pretty little head about Robert bringing Grant in to tear the place apart or about new business connections like the fashion show or about the whole comapny being sold. Im supposed to stick to my job and not ask questions, as if I didn't have any sense at all, didn't have anything to contribute to the decision-making process."

"Well"—Amy looked confused—"that's life."

"That's men." Nicole slapped her desk with the flat

of her palm. "No, it's me. I've let myself be exploited all my adult life. But not anymore."

"Wow." They listened to the hum of Seawinds starting up for the day: doors slamming, a cart trundling down to the stockroom, people's voices. Then Amy said, "But what about how you feel about Grant? You can't resign from that so easily."

"No, unfortunately."

The telephone rang. Amy answered it and told Edith Van Zandt that Nicole would return her call as soon as she came in.

Nicole said, "I've been alone a long time, but I never knew what solitude was until I fell in love with a man who doesn't love me."

"You're sure that's the way it is?"

"Yes, we had it out in Nassau." She rested her chin in her hands. "Is there an empty box or two around here? I need to pack some things."

"I was thinking that maybe Grant came back and bought Seawinds to be with you," Amy ventured.

"Only in the sense that he thinks he bought me, too. By day I run the company and by night I'm his devoted playmate. When he's here, that is. Most of the time he goes on leading his own life."

"This doesn't sound like you," Amy scolded. "It's bitter and twisted."

"And the hard part is," Nicole went on, "that I can't resist him. Whenever we're together it's wonderful, it's magic..." She put a hand to her forehead. "It doesn't fit with everything else. Oh, Amy, I'm so confused."

"Just do me one favor. Give yourself time to cool down. Don't do anything for a day or two. I'd really hate to see you go, Boss Lady. I'd miss you a lot."

"Thanks, kid."

Another group from Columbus Tours was due in two days, so Nicole spent an hour polishing the commentary for a second fashion show and writing in a part for a

male model, for which one of Amy's friends had agreed
to serve. She didn't know what else to do but to continue
working on pressing projects. Her resignation would have
to be preceded by an orderly transition. She wondered
who Grant could find for a new manager. Just before
ten, she heard people gathering in the studio and caught
a snatch of Grant's laughter. She turned on the radio to
block outside noise and went on working. Not Oregon,
she was thinking to herself half an hour later. After all
these years in the tropics she would be more comfortable
in a warm place. Santa Fe, perhaps? She'd heard that
many artists lived there. Maybe she could start a little
studio. It would be good to get back into the actual
batiking, as she'd started out, instead of doing admin-
istrative work all the time. She never had time these days
to design anything. In Santa Fe, she decided, she would
do wall hangings and pillows, so that she wouldn't have
to worry about clothing patterns and styles. In the beginning, that was. After business got going, she could
hire a seamstress. She would have a business all her
own, one that nobody could sell out from under her.

"Hello? Hello?"

The voice came from the reception area, around Amy's
desk. Nicole clicked off the radio and opened the door
to her office.

A woman stood by the desk. She was taller than Nicole, with the kind of spindly fine-boned good looks that
Nicole had always associated with private tennis courts
and horseback riding. Her simple but expensive print
skirt and lavender cotton sweater with pointelle detail
enhanced her ivory complexion and magnificent auburn
hair, which she wore swept up in a loose twist. Her neck
was as delicate as the stem of a champagne glass.

Nicole approached her with a sinking feeling. "Hi,
can I help you?"

"Yes, I hope so." The woman's smile was wide and

friendly. She was perhaps in her early thirties. "I'm looking for Grant Sutton." She was carrying an overnight bag, a purse made of harness leather, and a flat box wrapped in silver paper with a white bow. "He has arrived, hasn't he?"

"Yes, last night."

"Well, well." The woman looked around her. "The old boy's done all right for himself. This is a beautiful place. I was astonished when I drove up. It's bigger than I imagined from the way he described it to me."

"You've come to visit him?"

"Oh yes. But he isn't expecting me. It's a surprise. I just couldn't wait to see what he'd bought."

Another surprise. Just what I need, Nicole thought darkly. To the woman she explained, "Mr. Sutton is in a meeting right now. If you'd like to wait here, I'll tell him when he's finished. He shouldn't be much longer."

"That will be fine." The woman sat down in the captain's chair, balancing the box across her knees. "Please don't let me disturb your work."

"Who shall I say is here?"

"Susan Blair." The woman bit her lip, suppressing a smile.

"Would you like some coffee?"

"No, thanks."

What a gorgeous woman, Nicole thought, but then Grant probably didn't know any other kind. She went back to her desk and shuffled papers mindlessly until she heard voices coming from the direction of the studio. The woman, who had put the box on the floor and was reading a magazine, looked up and smiled as Nicole crossed the reception area.

Grant was lingering in the doorway of the studio, talking to several employees. "Hello," he said to Nicole, businesslike, as if he were seeing her for the first time that morning. "Glad to see you're still around. I think you and I have an appointment right now, in my office."

"I think you may want to keep another appointment first. There's someone here to see you."

"Who?"

"A woman named Susan Blair."

"Susan Blair?" Puzzled, he pulled at his mustache. "Oh, Susan Blair!" He broke into a huge grin. "Excuse me," he said to the group. "I'll talk to you later." He hastened off, chuckling to himself. Nicole followed with dragging feet.

When they got back to reception, Amy was at her desk, exchanging pleasantries with the visitor, who jumped out of her chair and held out her arms when Grant appeared.

He pounced on her and hugged her as if he had never in his life been so glad to see anyone. "Why didn't you let me know? I would have met your plane."

"Surprise, surprise. I thought you might not want me to come, at least not now."

"Are you serious? Any time is a good time."

Nicole had drifted to a halt beside Amy's desk. The two exchanged knowing glances.

"And he's only been here a few hours." Amy clucked.

Grant asked the woman, "How did you get away from Tony? Did you even tell him?"

"He went to Charlotte. He'll find out when he gets home. I left a note on the refrigerator. He'll fuss and fume, but he'll manage."

"Oh!" Amy exclaimed.

"I see you brought me a present." Grant picked up the gift box.

"It's just what you want," the woman said suggestively.

He held her at arm's length. "It's been a long time. Too long."

"I agree. That's why I came."

Nicole tried to fade into her office, but Grant called,

"There you are, Nicole. Come here. There's someone I'd like you to meet."

With a backward glance at Amy, she reluctantly joined the pair.

"This is Nicole Starr, Delia. Nicole, this is my sister."

CHAPTER TWELVE

"So you're Delia. I'm sorry. I thought—" Nicole floundered.

"The worst. She always thinks the worst," Grant broke in.

"But you said your name was something else," Nicole noted.

"Susan Blair is my horse's name." Delia laughed. "Grant tells me she's my alter ego. I didn't mean to be rude. It was merely a joke on big brother. Forgive me?" She had her brother's confidence in her own charm.

"It's all right."

"How long can you stay?" Grant wanted to know.

"Just the weekend. The kids are with Sarah." Delia waved an arm. "When do I get the grand tour?"

"After we've found you a place to say. Nicole, there are guest rooms, aren't there?"

"I'll tell Mamie to open one up." She couldn't resist

adding, "Since I have no other duties now, I'll be glad to get Delia settled."

"It's too bad your room isn't empty yet," Grant shot back. "Delia would like it."

Delia looked and listened, measuring them both.

"It will be available the next time she visits. Delia, I'd like you to meet my friend Amy and then we can go up to the house."

Later, as they crossed the patio, Nicole said to Delia, "You haven't seen your brother in a long time, I take it."

"No, he seldom gets home. But we keep in touch by phone. I've been handling the sale of his property in North Carolina for him."

"What property is that?"

"He had a piece of woodland with a cabin on it. He always joked that he'd retire there someday and live like Thoreau at Walden Pond, in solitary splendor. It's too bad he had to give it up."

"He told me about it once, but I didn't think it meant much to him."

They went inside. Delia said, "The land has sentimental value, because it belonged to our grandfather. Grant has trouble admitting that he cares about things. I don't know why, since he's so sure of himself in every other way. Maybe it has to do with the way he was brought up. I never once saw him cry as a child."

"Then why did he sell the land, if he cared about it?"

"He had to, to get the money to buy Seawinds."

They found Mamie in the pantry, dipping flour into a blue crockery bowl.

"Mamie, this is Mr. Sutton's sister."

"Delia Hopkins," Delia put in. "Nice to meet you."

"I don't know whether you've heard or not, but Mr. Sutton is the new owner of Seawinds," Nicole said.

"Oh yes," Mamie assured her, "Mr. Sutton told me himself when he brought his breakfast tray down."

"The tray . . ." Nicole blushed.

"It'll be nice to have him here," Mamie said to Delia. "This place has been too much for Mrs. Starr to run by herself. What I mean is, she has to work too hard. It needs a man, you know."

Nicole saw in the offing a comfortable monologue about the proper place for a woman, "Mamie, Mrs. Hopkins is here for the weekend. Do you think she could stay in Mrs. Gresham's old room?"

"Why yes, I aired it just last week. The bed is made up. I'll bring some towels."

Nicole led Delia to the ground-floor bed-sitting room, which was decorated in peach and apple green. "This is lovely," Delia said. "Grant told me that the former owner sold Seawinds as is, with all the furnishings."

"I wouldn't know. I wasn't in on the negotiations." Nicole drew back the curtains, opened a window, and turned on the ceiling fan. Delia took two dresses out of her suitcase and hung them in the closet. "Delia, why was your brother so determined to have Seawinds? I thought he didn't want to be tied down."

"He hasn't discussed that with you?"

"No, he hasn't."

Delia sat down at the dressing table, took pins out of her hair, and repositioned them. "I think it's part of a larger plan. But he'd have to tell you about it." She gave her hair a final pat. "I hope I'm not keeping you from your work. We can go back now."

"Oh, no. The fact is, I'm resigning my position here."

Delia turned around on the dressing table stool. Her large brown eyes shone with quickened interest. "Are you serious?"

"Perfectly serious." Nicole straightened the bedspread.

"This is marvelous. Absolutely marvelous." Her shoulders shook with suppressed laughter. Then she sobered up. "May I ask why?"

"It's complicated. But basically, your brother assumed he bought me when he bought the company. I'm showing him he didn't."

"Good for you. Do you have another job lined up?"

"Not yet. I'll probably go back to the States."

"I'd go farther. Go to Nepal, go to Australia, if you want to teach him a lesson."

"I'm not trying to teach him a lesson. I'm trying to save myself. Grant and I have been . . . close. I care about him. But I'm not a martyr. I've been through that before. I'm not going to give everything without getting as much in return."

"Are you in love with him?"

Nicole paused, but knew immediately that she could confide in Delia. "Yes, but that isn't enough. I used to think that love solved everything. By itself, it doesn't come close. There has to be more: respect, trust . . ."

They left the room together. Delia walked with her head bent, thinking. "My brother is a difficult man in a lot of ways. He's a lone wolf. He's selfish about sharing himself. But he's not a bad man and he's not an empty man."

"I know."

"I always hoped he would meet a woman like you, someone who would stand up to him and refuse to be manipulated, even if it meant losing him."

"When I told him I was resigning, he didn't protest."

Delia pursed her lips. "I'm sorry to hear that."

They recrossed the patio, which now smelled of sun-warmed jasmine.

"Wasn't Risa like that? Ready to stand up to him?" Nicole asked.

"No, Risa didn't leave out of love. I was never quite sure why she agreed to marry Grant in the first place. She was a nice person, but there were parts of Grant that she never took the trouble to understand. I suppose she married him for the outward qualities: his looks, the lifestyle he could afford, his social connections. But lots of people have those. She wasn't that interested in what made Grant Grant."

"Did she leave him for someone else?"

"No, but I think it was only a matter of time until her attention strayed. The word *forever* wasn't in her vocabulary. It's in his, though. That's why he hasn't leaped into marriage again." Her face saddened. "He's so cynical now. I hope it isn't too late for him."

"He's interviewed enough candidates, I understand."

"Yes, that's true, or it was true for a time." Delia smiled wanly. "You *are* teaching him a lesson, Nicole, and I'm grateful to you. I just hope it isn't costing you too much. And I hope he's still flexible enough to learn something." They arrived at the entrance to the offices. "I'm glad I met you."

"You're very easy to talk to. I feel as if I've known you a long time."

"Thanks." There was a pause, during which Nicole felt that Delia wanted to say more. But she only said, "I'll find my way from here. I'm sure we'll see each other later."

"Delia, you won't say anything to him about this talk, will you?"

"Oh no. Anyway, it wouldn't do any good. I know my brother. He'd rather let you go and pretend it doesn't matter than beg you to stay."

Back in her office, with the connecting door to Grant's office locked on her side, Nicole typed out a short letter of resignation and read it aloud. After some hesitation, she had made the resignation effective as of that day. Grant could figure things out on his own. The letter slipped from her fingers and skittered across the desk. Delia had confused her with her talk of teaching lessons. Everybody, including Grant and Amy, seemed to think she wasn't serious about leaving. But she was. Checkmated, she thought. Fold up the board. Put the pieces away.

She typed Grant's name on an envelope and sealed the letter in it. No sound came from the next room. People came and went outside her door, but no one telephoned or knocked. If was as if she had already left the premises. The long Bahamian lunch break came and went. When she heard Amy return from lunching with her boyfriend, Nicole went out with the letter.

"Is Grant around?"

"I think he took his sister to town. They're having lunch at the yacht club and then he has an appointment with the Van Zandts. He's been on the phone to the dye supplier."

"Didn't take him long to assume control, did it? Look, Amy, I'll be at the cottage if you need me. I just don't think I belong here today."

After she put the letter on Grant's desk, Nicole got her bicycle out of the storeroom, filled the basket with odds and ends she would need at the cottage, and set out. The road to the ocean, a shortcut across the interior of the island, was little more than a set of rocky, dusty tire tracks. The sun and pall of humidity sat over her like a gigantic steam iron. Several times she had to pull off into prickly undergrowth to let cars pass. By the time she got to the cottage, fiercely glad she had not used a Seawinds car, she was covered with a fine white dust and her teeth were gritty. Sweat trickled in her clothes.

She unlocked the door and went through the routine of putting supplies away and airing the place out. Rent or sell? she wondered, standing in the middle of the kitchen. Swiftly she went to the bedroom, changed into her bathing suit, and ran outside as if something were after her. She flung herself into the waves with a satisfying crash, swam straight out until she was tired, and then swam back with renewed fervor. Sitting in the shallows, letting the surf cream over her legs while she got her breath, she began to realize what she had done by resigning. Years of work thrown away to make a point. The waves sang *Sut-ton Sut-ton Sut-ton*.

What did Grant really think of her resignation? She didn't know. He had appeared not to care. Nicole splashed water over her shoulders. He was in a strangely high humor. Perhaps it was the euphoria of ownership. And she had thought that he made the trip to see her! She stood and plunged back into the waves.

She could always depend on the ocean. After an hour it had calmed the storm within her and washed her mind blank. But when she went back to the cottage, something had changed. Objects had more weight, a rounder command of space, as if they had acquired a new dimension. When she picked up a bottle of shampoo in the shower, her hand moved with a dancelike purity of line that quietly awed her. The unusual state continued while she dressed in shorts and a halter and fixed herself a glass of ice water. She knew a little about the Japanese tea ceremony and thought that she must be experiencing the oneness of being for which it strove. The glass of water at her lips was beautiful and pure in sensation and wholly sufficient to the moment. After the water was gone, she wanted to go on performing an action both useful and aesthetically pleasing; and she remembered that her guest room was empty, still waiting for her to paint the floor.

The paint she had bought was the blue of the evening sky after sundown: a tremulous, glowing blue on the edge of night. She opened the can and stirred the paint with a stick, watching the thick whirlpool of color form and reform under the movement of her hand. She laid out brushes and other necessities and began to paint along the baseboard of the wall opposite the door.

The work was slow and good. She let herself become lost in the action of her hand, spreading something of herself along with the paint. But gradually the moment began to unravel. Logic reasserted itself, along with a pain in her lower back. The cottage was timelessly precious this afternoon precisely because time was running out. She wasn't having a mystical experience; she was having an economic crisis. She could not both work at Seawinds and keep her dignity. She probably could not find another job in the precarious economy of Crescent Harbour. She could not keep the cottage without a job. Rent or sell? The painting became a chore.

The heat of late afternoon on the island was in some ways worse than the heat of midday, drier and more sterile. Nicole was sitting on her heels, wiping sweat out of her eyes, when her screen door creaked and Grant walked into the cottage. Stopping at the threshold of the guest room, he leaned against the doorjamb and folded his arms.

"Afternoon." He wore an old yellow polo shirt with faded cutoffs and he was barefoot.

"Don't you ever knock?"

"Not when I'm not welcome."

She went on painting, with her back to him. "Where's Delia?"

"I turned her over to a couple of the people in the studio—Betty and John, is it? She wanted to learn about batik. She's in purple dye up to her elbows and as happy as she can be."

"I like Delia."

"She was sorry you left."

"Please give her my apologies." He didn't pick up on that, so she knew he was going to let her stew in stifling silence for a while.

He did, while he whistled "For the Good Times." "I thought I'd find you here," he said at last. "That's the trouble with living on an island. When you want to run away, there's nowhere to go."

Nicole wrenched herself around and glared at him.

She tossed him a brush. "There. Go paint yourself into a corner."

"Thanks. I was feeling so useless." He came over to fill the brush with paint, then knelt somewhere behind her.

"Why aren't you at the office?" she challenged him.

"Why aren't you?"

"Didn't you find the letter I left on your desk?"

"Yes. I stamped it NULL AND VOID and filed it in the circular file."

"You can't do that." She slapped the brush down, spattered her knee, and cursed to herself. "It's unprofessional."

"You made your resignation effective as of today. You have to give two-weeks notice. Go look it up."

"All right. Two weeks. I'll write another letter tonight."

"Anything can happen in two weeks." He came to get more paint and went away again.

"Nothing's going to."

They painted in silence. Nicole remembered what Delia had said about Grant manipulating people to get what he wanted. She could feel her blood pressure rising.

"You'll have to fill out a form," he said, "stating, among other things, your reason for quitting."

"I'm quitting because I'm not going to be both a—a wage slave and your bed partner just because you assume it's going to be that way."

"Workers of the world, unite. Throw off your bed sheets."

"Stop making fun of me!"

"Well, if that's what you think I want, then it's true that this is double the work for the same pittance. I guess you had a better deal with old Robert."

"I was treated with dignity."

"You were treated with prurient cowardice."

"Okay, that's it." Nicole scrambled to her feet.

"How about if I raise your salary?"

"Get out."

"Sure. Looks like we're all done painting."

Nicole considered the floor. She had been moving backward on her knees, toward the door, as she painted. Behind her, Grant had painted very fast, also moving backward. She was standing on a narrow band of unpainted floor. He had cut off her exit. It was too far to jump.

"Very funny, Grant."

"I have an idea," he said from the doorway. "You can walk down that strip to the window and get out that way."

In a senseless fury, she shut the paint can and gathered up her supplies. When she got to the window, Grant was waiting outside. Tight-lipped, she handed out everything but her brush and he set the things along the base of the cottage. Then she went back and painted the strip until she was again at the window. She handed out her brush and sat down on the sill, swinging her legs out.

"Jump."

She jumped. He caught her and swung her up so that he ended with one arm under her knees and one arm under her shoulders. He started carrying her toward the ocean.

"What are you doing? Put me down."

"That's what I like about you, Nicole, you're such an optimist. But you don't have a prayer of my putting you down until I'm ready."

CHAPTER THIRTEEN

A BOSTON WHALER lay offshore, lashed to an old piling.

"Where are we going?" Nicole demanded.

He waded into the ocean with her. "Where I want to go. You don't have any choice in the matter." He was calmly determined in a way that was different from his usual combative arrogance. He dumped her in the boat, then went to untie the hawser. He came back, climbed in, and started the motor.

"Am I being abducted again?" she asked sarcastically.

"Not at all. We're still in office hours, according to the overtime you generally put in, and I want to talk business. Since you've threatened to resign—"

"It's not a threat. I mean it."

"Be that as it may. As the owner of Seawinds, I have the right to make you a counteroffer, to renegotiate the terms of your employment. Don't you agree?"

"Really, Grant, nothing you could say would make me stay. This is a charade."

"No, it isn't. No games, remember? I'm serious about this, Nicole. You owe me a hearing before you make a decision."

He *was* serious. She had never seen him so serious. "Well, all right. I guess I do owe you that much."

"Good. I'm glad to see you thinking of somebody besides yourself for a change."

"Thinking of myself? Why, for weeks I haven't thought of anyone but you."

"Hah." He hit the throttle and they were on their way.

They bent counterclockwise around the island, staying some fifty yards offshore. Grant drove fast and appeared to know exactly where he was going. In a few minutes they cut to the outside of Devil's Reef and headed for open water.

Nicole pointed back toward Silver Cay. "Aren't we going to town?"

The wind whipped away his reply.

She held onto her seat as they bucked across the waves at an angle. A few whitecaps showed and a waterspout was forming miles away. A curtain of rain hung over Turtle Cay. In the bottom of the boat were several boxes. She wondered what was in them. She wondered how a man like Grant had the nerve to imply that *she* was self-centered. She wondered about many things. They passed Shell Cay. The arc they had been traveling flattened out. The only land mass ahead of them would be a low spine of land called the Caves, for the shallow grottoes that had served as a rendezvous point for pirates in the colorful Bahamian past. It was uninhabited.

The wind scoured Grant's hair back and whipped ruddiness into his cheeks. His was the face of a man who knew what he wanted. She had thought that she knew his narrow wants, but now she was no longer sure. She herself still wanted the same thing. She would want Grant in Santa Fe or Oregon or Timbuktu or wherever she went.

But she'd rather not have him than have him on his own selfish terms. He caught her staring at him and grinned. Her heart swelled.

Nearly half an hour later, out of the deep rose the caves, an irregular gray line tinged with green, both welcoming and forbidding, like the shape of destiny.

Soon Grant cut the motor and they coasted in. "I discovered this place on my first visit to Silver Cay. It's a good place to be alone and think. No telephones, no interruptions. That also makes it a good neutral spot for negotiations."

"No conference table?"

"We'll make do. Here, you take the line and I'll get a couple of things we might need." He took along one of the boxes.

The sand of the narrow beach was pinkish and free of footprints. They started up the shore toward the grottoes, with Nicole feeling as if they were the only two people left in the world after some disaster. Grant's obvious seriousness of purpose only added to her melancholy. She would be no match for him in a closely reasoned argument.

The caves were around a point, facing the setting sun. Nicole stopped to look at the glorious sky, thinking of everything and nothing. Scarlet streamers waved in the water, weaving a royal highway westward. When she came to, Grant was building a fire in front of the first cave, out of some shattered crates that had washed ashore.

"Sorry." She went to join him.

"We have all the time in the world." He took a blanket out of the box and spread it by the fire. They sat down together.

"This is nice," she said after a stiff silence.

"Yes, it is. And I defy you to find a plane, taxi, bicycle, or any other means of escaping before we're through talking," he said with cool firmness.

She sifted sand through her fingers.

"What do you plan to do after you leave Seawinds?" he asked.

"I may start my own studio, somewhere in the Sunbelt. It will be small, no competition for you. I just want something of my own."

"You told me once that you'd never leave the island, that it was your paradise."

She went on sifting sand. "One of the characteristics of paradise is that nothing about it ever changes. Mine did. A stranger came, and now nothing will ever be the same again."

"Are you going to start that stranger business all over?"

She brushed sand off the blanket. "If you had remained a stranger," she resumed with difficulty, "I could have handled it. I could have shut you out so completely that my life could have gone on as it was. I'm good at shutting people out. I've done it lots of times." She coughed nervously. "I tried to get you out of my system in Nassau. That's one of the reasons I went. I thought that spending all that time with you and having an intense encounter would be like eating an entire chocolate cake by myself. I'd never want to touch chocolate cake again. I'd forgotten that sweets can be addictive."

Grant smiled, but sympathetically. "I'm glad to hear it."

"There's another reason why I went." She took a deep breath. Might as well throw the baby out with the bath. "I wanted to hurt you. You were so confident of your ability to charm me without yourself being affected. I wanted to show you what it felt like to be the one left behind. I'm ashamed of that. I had no business trifling with your feelings. Of all people, I should have known better."

The sunset flamed fleetingly in his eyes. He took her hand, turned it over, and smoothed the lines in her palm, one by one, with a thumb. "You're not making a very convincing argument for moving to the Sunbelt."

"Don't you understand? You're against a developing relationship. When I said I love you, you said I was confused. You want me when you want me and not any other time. You're counting on me to work myself to a frazzle at Seawinds, even though you were the one who showed me that I was being exploited."

"It's all an old story, one you've lived through before."

She bowed her head. "I got what I deserved for trying to hurt you. You were unaffected, but I fell in love. I destroyed that distance between us that kept you a stranger. Now I love you the way my eyes are green. It's a part of me that will never change. But I won't be used again, not in business and not in love. Not by anybody."

Grant punched up the fire. "Well, if your story of our relationship were true, you would be right to leave. But let me tell you a different story. Remember, negotiations have at least two sides.

"When I met you that first afternoon at the airport, you were like a ripe pear waiting to be plucked, with no more idea of what you had to offer than a pear has. That unconscious sensuality and intelligence intrigued me. I pushed too hard and got the expected brushoff. That evening after dinner at Gresham's, you rebuffed me again. Normally I would have said to hell with the lady and cut my losses." He leaned back on an elbow and stretched his legs out, crossing them at the ankles. "But I kept discovering further depths to you, beneath your office personality. The night we had dinner at the Coral Reef was a turning point. We connected. But you ran away again. That was it, for me. I took the offer to leave the island early. But I thought of you every day I was gone. Finally I realized that it wasn't finished for us. I wanted you, and not just physically. I wanted to know everything about you. But the only way you could ever really belong to me would be for you to free yourself from the chains of the past."

The sun was gone, but its splendor still hung in the sky. The wind had freshened. Sitting cross-legged, Nicole moved instinctively closer to Grant and her thigh settled against his ribs. He was the warmest thing in the wide world, warmer than the fire.

"But that morning at the cottage, before we left for Nassau, you practically told me that Nassau would be the end."

"I don't know that I can justify having said that. I wanted you the way a man dying of thirst wants water. It was a crazy feeling and unsettling for a rational man. Besides, being alone and proud of it is the only way of life I've known for years. Things were developing fast. For both our sakes, they had to be slowed down." He pointed an index finger at her. "Also, you insisted you wanted it that way."

"Yes, I did shut you out."

"That was the other problem and it was a serious one. Those chains of yours wouldn't stay broken. We had one good night, but by the next morning I was just another wandering, philandering charmer to you."

"In other words, 'alone and proud of it,'" Nicole reminded him.

"That doesn't mean I enjoy hurting people. I don't. I play straight with people's emotions. I tried to play straight with yours."

"Then those things you said to me at the restaurant—that I was the woman you had been looking for, and the rest—they were true?"

"Every word."

"I was so busy protecting myself." She shook her head. "That's what you meant when you said I only think of myself, isn't it?"

He pulled her down beside him and put his arms

around her. "You were on a delayed rebound from your marriage. I wanted to possess you completely, not have you fall in love with me just because I was the first man you saw when you woke up from that long sleep of widowhood. You needed more time, that's all."

"I kept comparing you to Barry. That couldn't have helped."

"It angered me," he said slowly, "when you looked at me and saw his face. Yet that was your most desperate defense against me. Deep down you were afraid of me or, rather, terrified of the feelings we shared. They were too raw and powerful. So if you could make me over into another Barry, you could convince yourself to leave me alone." He took her face in his hands. "Look at me. Recognize me for what I am: a new man in your life, a man who loves you."

"You love me?" She smiled tremulously and could barely see his answering smile in the gathering twilight.

"I do. Can you figure out the moral of the story I've been telling you? You chose to see me as a man who would keep leaving you. But I keep coming back to you. Over and over, no matter where you run or when, I come back to you. And now I've come back for good. I told you that last night. Nicole, I'm tired of traveling, tired of spending Christmas in hotels and of celebrating my birthdays alone on airplanes or with strangers. And I need you."

"What about your consulting business?"

"I'm cutting back on it, because of the work here. But when I go on a business trip, I want you to go with me. There's a whole world out there to experience together." He pulled the cardboard box over and took from it the silver-wrapped package that Delia had brought. "This is for you." While Nicole unwrapped the box, he went on, "I've been looking for a place to settle down for a year or so. I hadn't been here two days before I knew this was it. I didn't expect to fall in love, too." He cleared his throat. "That's hard for me to say, because I take love seriously, maybe too seriously. But it's getting easier to say it. I love you, Nicole."

"It's not just convenient to love me because I happen to live in the place where you want to settle down?" she asked with gentle archness.

"Love is a lot of things, but it isn't convenient."

"I love you, too. You alone."

"I know that now. Well, go on and finish opening your present. It's something I arranged for Delia to have made up at Sutton Fabrics in North Carolina. It's one of a kind."

Nicole folded back tissue paper and lifted out a filmy peignoir of semi-sheer cotton edged with what appeared to be handmade lace. She held it near the fire to examine the design. On a background of white, printed in the particular purple of iris, floated ethereal shapes of butterflies and flowers. On the wings of every butterfly, in whimsical script, was printed *marry me*.

"I wrote that little message myself," Grant volunteered. "It's short but it has a nice ring, don't you think? Marry me?"

The box slid from her lap as Nicole slipped into his embrace and they rolled together on the blanket. "Yes, I'll marry you, Mr. Sutton."

The fire snapped and hissed. And hissed and snapped.

"Happy?" he whispered against her cheek.

"This is more than happiness."

"I'll say. It's arousal, too."

"But will you be happy giving up your old life?" she asked.

"I was ready to give it up. Besides, you changed; why can't I? Think I'm too old?" Their lips met. "I've found a home that I never want to leave, and it isn't a building. It's you."

Their legs twined, his viselike around hers. "Why is falling in love this second time so difficult and so unbearably exquisite at once?" Nicole sighed.

"It'd be difficult the first time, too, if people could realize what was happening to them. Tender youth is protected by ignorance." He raised himself on one elbow and combed her hair out on the blanket with his fingers, making a golden halo. "That first love could never be as deep as this." He spread the halo wider. "Remember that other surprise I said I had for you, the one you didn't want to hear about?"

"You mean this wasn't it?"

"I had the Van Zandts draw up some new papers concerning the ownership of Seawinds. They're waiting to hear from you before they make an official document to receive signatures. That is, if you have any interest at all in being a joint owner..."

Her eyes misted as she clasped him to her.

"No need to give me an answer right now." He chuckled and kissed her throat.

"How could I ever have doubted you? How could—"

His mouth covered hers, pressing her lips apart for his tongue to enter. Wood shifted on the fire and sparks danced up to the sky.

"Shouldn't we be getting back?" she murmured reluctantly. "What about Delia?"

"Delia can take care of herself." He pulled down the straps of her halter and kissed her bare shoulders. "She'll be glad I'm not letting you get away. She likes you as much as I told her she would. She was furious with me this morning."

"Did she give you good advice?"

"No adivce at all." Grant threw back his head and laughed. "She merely called me a horse's rear. And Delia knows her horses." He laughed again. "No man is a hero to his sister."

"You always were a wicked man with a cliché." She laughed. "But don't we want to tell her our news right away?"

His hand found the zipper of her shorts. "Do you really want to leave this very minute?"

"Well, maybe not right...now." She gasped as his hand slid inside.

"Besides, m'love, there's something I haven't told you about the boat. We can't make it back. We're nearly out of gas."

"What?" She tried to sit up, but he pushed her down.

"Relax. I planned it that way."

They didn't talk for a while.

"Well, well," Nicole said in a breathy voice, "the old out-of-gas ploy."

"Mmmm. My way of demonstrating very concretely that we're together now for good."

"I hope the boat has a radio."

"It does, when we need help. Ah, that's good...You're all the help I need at the moment."

For a time the fire and the ocean talked to each other.

With his head pillowed on her breasts, he asked, "You're not just marrying me to get half of Seawinds, are you?"

"I accepted your proposal before I knew that, remember? But there are still lots of unanswered questions." She ran her fingers through his hair. "Are you just marrying me to avoid trying to find a new manager? And...what about children?"

He raised up to look at her. "I guess we'll have to enter into further negotiations."

"Is *that* what we're doing?"

"Might take a while. But I brought food and blankets."

Nicole smiled up at the stars. Then, as their mouths met again, she could no longer see the stars. But she could feel them inside her, spinning and singing.

WATCH FOR 6 NEW TITLES EVERY MONTH!

Second Chance at Love

____	06540-4	FROM THE TORRID PAST #49 Ann Cristy
____	06544-7	RECKLESS LONGING #50 Daisy Logan
____	05851-3	LOVE'S MASQUERADE #51 Lillian Marsh
____	06148-4	THE STEELE HEART #52 Jocelyn Day
____	06422-X	UNTAMED DESIRE #53 Beth Brookes
____	06651-6	VENUS RISING #54 Michelle Roland
____	06595-1	SWEET VICTORY #55 Jena Hunt
____	06575-7	TOO NEAR THE SUN #56 Aimée Duvall
____	05625-1	MOURNING BRIDE #57 Lucia Curzon
____	06411-4	THE GOLDEN TOUCH #58 Robin James
____	06596-X	EMBRACED BY DESTINY #59 Simone Hadary
____	06660-5	TORN ASUNDER #60 Ann Cristy
____	06573-2	MIRAGE #61 Margie Michaels
____	06650-8	ON WINGS OF MAGIC #62 Susanna Collins
____	05816-5	DOUBLE DECEPTION #63 Amanda Troy
____	06675-3	APOLLO'S DREAM #64 Claire Evans
____	06689-3	SWEETER THAN WINE #78 Jena Hunt
____	06690-7	SAVAGE EDEN #79 Diane Crawford
____	06692-3	THE WAYWARD WIDOW #81 Anne Mayfield
____	06693-1	TARNISHED RAINBOW #82 Jocelyn Day
____	06694-X	STARLIT SEDUCTION #83 Anne Reed
____	06695-8	LOVER IN BLUE #84 Aimée Duvall
____	06696-6	THE FAMILIAR TOUCH #85 Lynn Lawrence
____	06697-4	TWILIGHT EMBRACE #86 Jennifer Rose
____	06698-2	QUEEN OF HEARTS #87 Lucia Curzon
____	06851-9	A MAN'S PERSUASION #89 Katherine Granger
____	06852-7	FORBIDDEN RAPTURE #90 Kate Nevins
____	06853-5	THIS WILD HEART #91 Margarett McKean
____	06854-3	SPLENDID SAVAGE #92 Zandra Colt
____	06855-1	THE EARL'S FANCY #93 Charlotte Hines
____	06858-6	BREATHLESS DAWN #94 Susanna Collins
____	06859-4	SWEET SURRENDER #95 Diana Mars
____	06860-8	GUARDED MOMENTS #96 Lynn Fairfax
____	06861-6	ECSTASY RECLAIMED #97 Brandy LaRue
____	06862-4	THE WIND'S EMBRACE #98 Melinda Harris
____	06863-2	THE FORGOTTEN BRIDE #99 Lillian Marsh
____	06864-0	A PROMISE TO CHERISH #100 LaVyrle Spencer
____	06866-7	BELOVED STRANGER #102 Michelle Roland
____	06867-5	ENTHRALLED #103 Ann Cristy
____	06869-1	DEFIANT MISTRESS #105 Anne Devon
____	06870-5	RELENTLESS DESIRE #106 Sandra Brown
____	06871-3	SCENES FROM THE HEART #107 Marie Charles
____	06872-1	SPRING FEVER #108 Simone Hadary
____	06873-X	IN THE ARMS OF A STRANGER #109 Deborah Joyce
____	06874-8	TAKEN BY STORM #110 Kay Robbins
____	06899-3	THE ARDENT PROTECTOR #111 Amanda Kent

All of the above titles are $1.75 per copy

SK-41a

Available at your local bookstore or return this form to:

 SECOND CHANCE AT LOVE
Book Mailing Service
P.O. Box 690, Rockville Centre, NY 11571

Please send me the titles checked above. I enclose _____ Include 75¢ for postage
and handling if one book is ordered; 25¢ per book for two or more not to exceed
$1.75. California, Illinois, New York and Tennessee residents please add sales tax.

NAME_____

ADDRESS_____

CITY_____STATE/ZIP_____

(allow six weeks for delivery)   SK-41b

NEW FROM THE PUBLISHERS OF *SECOND CHANCE AT LOVE!*

To Have and to Hold™

__**THE TESTIMONY #1** by Robin James (06928-0)
*After six dark months apart, dynamic Jesse Ludan is a coming home
to his vibrant wife Christine. They are united by shared thoughts
and feelings, but sometimes they seem like strangers as they struggle
to reaffirm their love.*

__**A TASTE OF HEAVEN #2** by Jennifer Rose (06929-9)
*Dena and Richard Klein share a life of wedded bliss...until Dena
launches her own restaurant. She goes from walking on air to walking
on eggs—until she and Richard get their marriage cooking again.*

__**TREAD SOFTLY #3** by Ann Cristy (06930-2)
*Cady Densmore's love for her husband Rafe doesn't dim during the
dangerous surgery that restores his health, or during the long campaign
to reelect him to the Senate. But misunderstandings threaten the very
foundation of their marriage.*

__**THEY SAID IT WOULDN'T LAST #4** by Elaine Tucker (06931-0)
*When Glory Mathers, a successful author, married Wade Wilson,
an out-of-work actor, all the gossips shook their heads. Now, ten years
later, Wade is a famous film star and Glory feels eclipsed...*

__**GILDED SPRING #5** by Jenny Bates (06932-9)
*Kate yearns to have Adam's child, the ultimate expression of their abiding
love. But impending parenthood unleashes fears and uncertainties
that threaten to unravel the delicate fabric of their marriage.*

__**LEGAL AND TENDER #6** by Candice Adams (06933-7)
*When Linny becomes her lawyer husband's legal secretary, she's
sure that being at Wes's side by day...and in his arms at night...can only
improve their marriage. But misunderstandings arise...*

__**THE FAMILY PLAN #7** by Nuria Wood (06934-5)
*Jenny fears domesticity may be dulling her marriage, but her struggles
to expand her horizons—and reawaken her husband's desire—provoke
family confusion and comic catastrophe.*

All Titles are $1.95

Available at your local bookstore or return this form to:

 SECOND CHANCE AT LOVE!
Book Mailing Service
P.O. Box 690, Rockville Centre, NY 11571

Please send me the titles checked above. I enclose _____ Include 75¢ for postage and
handling if one book is ordered; 25¢ per book for two or more not to exceed $1.75. California,
Illinois, New York and Tennessee residents please add sales tax.

NAME_____

ADDRESS_____

CITY_____ STATE/ZIP_____

(allow six weeks for delivery)   THTH #67

WHAT READERS SAY ABOUT
SECOND CHANCE AT LOVE BOOKS

"I can't begin to thank you for the many, many hours of pure bliss I have received from the wonderful SECOND CHANCE [AT LOVE] books. Everyone I talk to lately has admitted their preference for SECOND CHANCE [AT LOVE] over all the other lines."
—S. S., Phoenix, AZ*

"Hurrah for Berkley . . . the butterfly and its wonderful SECOND CHANCE AT LOVE."
—G. B., Mount Prospect, IL*

"Thank you, thank you, thank you—I just had to write to let you know how much I love SECOND CHANCE AT LOVE . . . "
—R. T., Abbeville, LA*

"It's so hard to wait 'til it's time for the next shipment . . . I hope your firm soon considers adding to the line."
—P. D., Easton, PA*

"SECOND CHANCE AT LOVE is fantastic. I have been reading romances for as long as I can remember—and I enjoy SECOND CHANCE [AT LOVE] the best."
—G. M., Quincy, IL*

*Names and addresses available upon request